Sidetracked Love

A Eusebeia's Pets MC Story

MariaLisa deMora

Editing: Hot Tree Editing

First Published 2025

ISBN 13: 978-1-946738-83-7

DEDICATION

"Sometimes two people have to fall apart to realize how much they need to fall back together"

~ *Colleen Hoover*

This book is dedicated to everyone who had a period of pause in their life, and then picked up all the pieces and moved forward anyway. Whether that's a lost love, a stalled career, or health challenges. Go you.

Contents

ACKNOWLEDGMENTS

2024 … What a year, amirite?

I won't detail everything here, mostly because I'd rather forget 2024 existed. I got sick, had multiple surgeries, found out that ongoing health issues were likely permanent, and learned how to ask for help. (Not really, that one's a work in progress.)

This story was originally published in an anthology back in 2023. I'm glad to finally be in a position to expand it dramatically and bring the full story to y'all.

Will there be a second Eusebeia's Pets story? Maybe … prolly!

Woofully yours,

~ML

Sidetracked Love

Mya Taylor long ago decided kids in high school shouldn't be allowed to make life-altering decisions. Of course, that was only after she'd left her first love and hometown behind in the same move, determined to relegate both to the past. That worked well enough until years later, in rolled that same first love, sweeping in to rescue her in dramatic fashion.

Kade Martinez had loved only one person in his life, and she'd walked away a long time ago. Then, when Mya turned up again, thousands of miles and two decades later, it seemed like fate. Will they manage to put their pain and hurt behind them to explore the heat that still sparks between them?

Prologue

Mya

The air in Mya Taylor's childhood home always carried a faint tang of despair. That, paired with the ever-present stale beer, unwashed laundry, and the sharp bite of her father's anger, lingered like a ghost even when he wasn't around. It clung to the walls of their sagging farmhouse, a relic of better days when the fields out back still bloomed with corn instead of weeds.

By seventeen, Mya had learned to navigate that house as if it were an active battlefield, stepping light to avoid the creak of the third stair, knowing which corners hid the echoes of her mother's quiet sobs. She'd long ago decided that kids shouldn't be saddled with choices that could break their lives apart. Especially ones still fumbling through high school. Yet there she was, standing at the edge of one, her heart a tangled knot of love and fear.

Kade Martinez was her anchor in that storm, the boy one road over whose laughter could cut through the thickest gloom. They'd met years back, two kids chasing fireflies across the pasture that stretched between their homes, barefoot and fearless. Over time, that pasture wore a path connecting their worlds, one beaten flat by sneakers and bike tires. Kade's house was a refuge, a place where the air smelled of his mom's cooking instead of regret, where his little brother Riley's chatter drowned out the silence Mya carried home.

She loved him before she even knew what love meant, a slow burn that grew from shared secrets whispered under the oak tree to the ache that bloomed when she caught his hazel eyes lingering on her a beat too long.

But love, she learned, wasn't simple. No, it couldn't be, not when it tangled with the chaos of her life. Her father's drinking had worsened that final year, his fists finding her mother's skin more often than the bottle. Mya's part-time job wages vanished into his pockets, and the expectation loomed that she'd stay, work full-time after graduation, and keep the family afloat. Kade, though, had become her imagination's escape hatch, her what-if. She'd planned to tell him at prom, to spill the truth of her feelings under the dim glow of fairy lights, hoping he'd say it back. She'd rehearsed it a hundred times, her palms sweaty as she finally asked him, voice trembling but sure.

His no had hit like a punch. "Can't, Mya. I'm goin' with Paul," he'd said, eyes shadowed with something she couldn't read. Paul, the quarterback with a swagger and a secret he'd only just begun to own. Mya didn't ask why—didn't dare—because the rejection carved a wound too deep to probe. She pulled back, let the distance grow, convinced Kade's choice meant he'd never see her the way she saw him. Gay, she thought, the unspoken word a wall between them, built from her own assumptions. She didn't know then that Kade was wrestling his own truths, caught between supporting a friend and the unspoken pull he felt toward her.

Graduation came, a blur of caps and gowns, and Mya made her move. She'd applied to a university three thousand miles away in secret, her grades and a scholarship her ticket out. The night after the ceremony, while her parents slept off another fight, she packed her bags into the beat-up pickup she'd bought with saved-up tips. She didn't leave a note. Not at home, and for sure not anywhere else. She didn't trust anyone not to stop her. Kade most of all. She couldn't face his deep brown eyes, couldn't risk him talking her into staying. So she drove, tears often blurring the road, until the ocean stretched before her, vast and wild, promising a life free of fists and shouting.

*****

Kade

Kade, stood in the wreckage Mya had left behind. Watching from his bedroom window as she'd packed the truck and then peeled out, he'd run outside only to stand in the dust cloud that had swallowed her taillights. From that day forward, his notebooks were filled with unsaid words. He'd poured all his anger, hurt, and the depth of a love he hadn't known how to voice into those pages.

As time went by, and Mya hadn't returned, things turned south for the Martinez family. His mother was diagnosed during his brother Riley's senior year. So Kade stayed in that dying town, tethered by his brother and a mother fading under cancer's weight, strumming a guitar in dive bars until the dream soured. Mother in the ground, brother overseas … it was time.

Past time.

When he finally left, it was with a motorcycle between his legs and no patched vest on his back, not back then. Mya had been mentioned in the class newsletter as being in the medical field on the West coast, so that was the direction he aimed the bike. When he finally hit the coast, he took in a long breath tasting of salt and water, and it eased tension inside him. He was where she was, and that wasn't a coincidence nor was it a mistake. He just knew.

The next weeks were spent learning the layout of the land. He studied for and passed the exams needed for an ambulance driver, and the work seemed to suit him. Helping people was what he did best. He locked in additional classes and certifications, moving from the front seat to the back of the meat wagon.

Every day off saw him on his bike, riding up and down the roads of the coast. Proximity matters, because that meant he'd made multiple contacts in Eusebeia's Pets MC. Months passed and he finally asked for a patch, and the way the club members circled around him reinforced his decision. Over the next couple of years, the club became the family he'd lost.

Two decades on from that prom that never happened, he had no idea of the twists that fate—or dumb luck—was going to pull. A car crash on a coastal road, Kade's voice cut through the chaos and he stepped forwards, helping pull an injured woman from the wreckage.

When she stood in front of him Kade had to look twice.

It was Mya.

His Mya.

The sparks that flew between them weren't gone. The attraction, and the love, had been waiting for a moment like this.

One thing was clear: their story wasn't over.

It was just beginning.

Chapter One

Mya Taylor woke slowly, gradually becoming aware of her surroundings. That was nearly overshadowed by the way her head was hurting. Not as if she'd simply gotten drunk, but more. Much more. As she focused on the discomfort, the ache swelled into a deeper throb that threatened to roil her stomach.

Ugh.

To test the extent of the pain, she tentatively moved her head from side to side.

With a start, Mya realized she'd been feeling warm huffs of air fanning comfortingly across the back of her neck. It was someone's sleeping breath. She'd been aware of the sensation but not concerned, which was entirely unlike her.

She froze in place before her normal early morning stretch could move her limbs more than a fraction of an inch. Holding her breath, she listened intently. There was no other sound, nothing but the soft rustle of air moving regularly in and out of someone's lungs. The rest of the house was quiet and still.

Opening her eyes wide, wincing at the sudden stab of pain, Mya darted her gaze around the room, gratefully taking in the familiar walls filled with photos of her extended—and very far away—family.

She was at home, in her own bedroom.

That's good news.

And someone was sharing her bed.

Less good news.

Mya didn't bring lovers home. Ever. Not that she had too many of those. Short-term or not. In fact, her last serious relationship had been back in the first years of college, which now seemed a world away.

What's going on? Who the hell is it?

Fear made her pounding head swim, and she struggled to keep her breathing under control. She won the fight, but just barely.

Do. Not. Panic.

No matter what she told herself, the rapid thudding of her heart rattling her ribcage shared the true story. But panic wouldn't help things. It never did. No matter how hard her body fought to leap away, she needed to stay calm. Pulling a slow breath in, she dialed in on what she could see and feel.

Okay. What we're going to do now is assess, then address, and deescalate if necessary. Slow and steady. Step by step.

Getting her head into work mode helped considerably. As her breaths came a little more freely, she turned her attention to everything she could know without disturbing her company.

The heavy weight of a massive arm lay draped across her body. Without moving her head, she could just make out a tattooed elbow hinged to fit snuggly around her ribs.

Lower, there was a heated touch against her skin, which she thought was a hand where her waist met the mattress, effectively trapping her against what felt like a long, strong body.

Muscled, tattooed, and physically substantial.

More warm flesh pressed firmly against her back, from the base of her neck to the top of her buttocks, and a slow, guarded glance down her length showed her torso clad in bra and panties. The mattress was hot underneath her, but the room air cool on her exposed legs, sheets having been kicked away.

Continuing to carefully modulate her breathing, Mya wrung every cell of her brain, trying to remember what events had led to her being in this position. She came up with little at first, and, with a growing sense of returning panic, attempted to dig deeper.

She remembered smirking at her best friend as the bouncer called them out of the raucous crowd already lined up and impatiently waiting to enter the club. She and Karen had sauntered inside with little flirty twitches of their hips, walk-dancing to the beat that escaped from the now-opened front doors. They weren't frequent fliers at the club but came often enough that they were both comfortable here.

The club had been busy, which meant Mya and Karen had to wait in line for their first drinks, still dancing in place before finally reaching the head of the queue and ordering two cocktails each so they wouldn't have to come back as soon. Afterward, there'd been some slightly awkward dancing, with both hands full of sloshing ice and liquid, so Mya had quickly downed the first drink. She clearly remembered more dancing and finishing the second drink, then begging off more alcohol.

I wasn't drunk. Couldn't have been. Not nearly. Not off two watered-down cocktails.

Mya had just wanted to dance.

Later, a sweaty Karen brought her a bottle of water. Upon inspection, it had been still sealed, so Mya hadn't hesitated to open and upend it. *Safety first, always.* She'd drained the bottle in seconds. Like Karen, her clothes and hair were drenched with salty liquid from her exertions.

Things after that stayed clear, and she held memories of the club's interior finally brightening as last call was shouted across the room. She'd booked them a car from an app on her phone, and one rideshare later, a still-grinning Karen had been dropped at the door of her apartment building, the vehicle smoothly pulling away from the curb and into traffic as Mya waved goodbye.

Mya was yanked from her memories when she moved slightly and a section of her arm made itself known, stinging from the contact with the bedding. She lifted her arm and stared at the broad scrape, also noticing bruises crossing her chest from shoulder to hip, the line of blue and purple partially obscured by the tattoo-lined arm still tucked firmly around her body.

That's a seat belt bruise.

Ignoring that information and closing her eyes, Mya tried to recapture the thread of what had happened last night.

During the ride, still about a block from her small bungalow home, there'd been a sound. In retrospect, she recognized it as sliding tires on pavement. Then the car jolted violently and abruptly lifted to one side, rolling quickly until everything was upside down before coming to a sudden stop. A post appeared like magic right in front of Mya's face, the force of the collision against the structure crushing the door in towards where she sat and smashing the glass, shards spraying directly at her face. She'd thrown her arms up to ward off the shiny shrapnel. Then everything went black.

She'd come to hanging upside down, and confused, she'd stayed in that position for a moment before scrabbling for the button to release the belt holding her in place. Somewhere nearby, there was a shout.

That's where things went dim again. She remembered striking her head hard against the inside of the car when she fell, and had vaguely heard groaning from the front seat, likely the college student who'd been driving the car. But she didn't think she'd passed out again.

Memories of bright lights and loud siren sounds meshed in a painful cacophony that again bounced around inside her brain.

The door opposite where she'd lay crumpled had been wrenched open with a squeal of tortured metal, and then arms had reached through the opening. People in uniforms were crowding the space, each issuing a different command. Through all the confusion in her head, it was the tone of a single familiar voice that triggered a new memory, overriding the multiple voices and telling her to stay still, that they'd get her out. For an instant, she'd been a child again, following the back tire of her best friend's bike as they rode through the woods on a deer trail.

She'd shaken that off and, ignoring all their suggestions, had rolled to a low crouch and duckwalked her way to the open door. That single voice had spoken again, chiding her to be careful, to watch her head, to take it slow, and when she'd made it to the street and stood upright, the face matching the voice hadn't been what she'd expected.

Growing up as Mya had out in the country, kids couldn't be picky about who their friends were. Anyone living within a mile or so was typically considered viable playmates regardless of age differences, and most friendships made in this way lasted decades. Those were the kind of friends where months or years could pass without a visit, and still conversations would be free and easy the instant contact was renewed.

Kade Martinez had lived one road over, and after the first time they'd met, there'd soon been a beaten path through the pastures and woods between their houses. Mya had been as comfortable at Kade's house as she had her own. More comfortable, maybe. They'd been besties.

The familiar and reassuring voice had belonged to him. Here. Thousands of miles away from where they'd both grown up. And now, just at the moment when she needed comfort and steadiness in the worst way, he'd appeared as if summoned from thin air.

Mya now lay on the soft mattress, held in place against the large male body behind her, and tried to remember the last time she'd seen Kade. High school definitely, and most probably the day of their graduation.

She hadn't told any of her classmates her plans, knowing they'd leak the info to someone, and then her parents would find out. Or worse, Kade might. Either could have been catastrophic.

Her parents had made their expectations clear. She should start working full-time immediately, with her paychecks being signed over just as her part-time job wages had been. And Kade? Well, it had just been better that way. A clean break.

The day after their graduating class had walked the stage, shaking hands with school officials and confidently moving tassels from one side to the other, Mya had shoved her already packed bags into the small pickup truck bought in her name, and driven away, headed for a summer semester of classes in a university on the other edge of the country. Her grades and interests earning her a full-ride scholarship to a place no one would suspect she'd known about, much less applied to.

That long drive had been full of doubt and worry, and pain as she grieved for her best friend, Kade. But then, from the first moment she'd seen the ocean, its uneven roiling surface lined with waves riding into the coastline and up the sands, the sound of birds and wind and life—she'd been hooked. It was as different from home as it could be, and she'd loved it.

No shouting, no lifted fists—just the serenity of the water.

By the time she'd been ready for post-graduate work, her match for a residency program had shifted her barely farther down the coast from those first years. Eventually, she'd decided she liked the new city well enough to accept a position in a practice that wound up being just a few blocks down the street from her little rental house.

Now, here she was, three thousand-odd miles away and two decades later, apparently fully embedded in one of the best fantasies her teenaged self could have ever imagined.

In bed with Kade Martinez. Who'd have thought?

As she'd stood next to the mangled car, staring up into those soft brown eyes she'd once tried to count all the amber flecks in, the man—Kade—had lost his composure for only a moment before a smooth and confident professional persona had clicked into place.

For that barest moment, she'd seen raw pain and banked anger cross his features, those plush lips she'd imagined kissing a thousand times flexing into a straight white line. The scruff along his jawline was new, and Mya found she didn't mind it at all, as the trimmed evidence of his maturity framed his face well. With his tattooed hand under her elbow, she'd allowed Kade to steer her to the back of an ambulance, taking a seat on the bumper at his quiet request.

The pounding in her temples renewed suddenly, and Mya groaned softly, letting the memory flow away for now.

At the sound, the man behind her stirred, his arm tightening around her ribs for a second, fingers curling against her skin.

Kade Martinez was in her bed.

Surreal.

Kade, who'd turned down her stumbling invitation to their senior prom, and took the football quarterback instead.

Kade, who she'd loved since before she'd even understood what the emotion twisting through her chest meant.

The boy she'd run from.

"Mya?" His voice held a truckload of rasp, gravelly with disuse and sleep. The fact he immediately knew who she was should be a plus, but there'd been too many years for it to tease her hopes more than a tickle. "How's the head, honey?"

"Manageable. I think I need something to eat and then to take some painkillers. I've got some OTC stuff in the bathroom." She wiggled away from him, creating space between their bodies. His arm tightened at first, then relaxed, his forearm, then wrist, and finally, his large hand trailing across her ribs. "I was surprised to see you last night."

And I don't remember why you're here. But we'll ignore that for now.

"I've been in town a couple years." The mattress moved as if he'd shrugged. "Didn't know where you'd landed after school." His hand slipped back around her waist, and he tugged slightly. "Let me see your face, Mya. See what the bruising looks like."

"How am I here instead of the hospital?" She held her breath before letting it out in a rush. "I remember sitting on the ambulance, but really nothing past that."

"You were talking a mile a minute but seemed coherent enough most of the time. It's concerning you don't remember now." The tug came again, more insistent this time. "Come on, turn over, honey."

Mya shifted to her back slowly, the movement waking more pain all through her body. Shoulders, arms, ribs, hips—it seemed like everything hurt right now. But her head was worst of all, pounding in time with her heartbeat, racing along at speed.

"Oh, Mya." Kade's eyes shifted, looking back and forth across her face before moving to take in the bruising across her chest. "You got slammed around but good." He grimaced. "Well, bad, but you know what I mean. Let me look." His hand drifted from her belly to her hips, and fresh goose bumps broke out on her arms when the chill air hit a span of flesh previously covered by her panties. "Yeah, hips too. You're lucky you didn't break anything."

"Except my head. That seems pretty broken." She flexed her fingers. "Everything's sore. We weren't even going that fast."

"No, but the guy who ran into you was. Well over the limit, both speed and alcohol. Cops took him in, and from the way they talked, he's a frequent flier." Kade's head shook side to side. "How someone could put innocent people at risk like that is beyond me."

"Addicts have a skewed sense of reality, and once they're under the influence, their decision-making capabilities reflect that perception. He's probably repeatedly told everyone he knows that he's fine, and he likely believed he was fine last night too." In her practice, she saw the fallout from that kind of behavior all the time. "It's hard to feel compassion, but as with any mental condition, the disruptive behavior is driven by the—sorry, that's me going into full lecture mode. Sorry."

"No worries," he said softly, his gaze drifting across her face again. His mouth twisted to the side. "I remember your daddy all too well."

"I try not to talk about him." She softened the chastisement with a small smile. "Except to my therapist, of course."

"You're in medicine, right?" Kade shifted, folding an arm under his head, using his bicep as a pillow. "That's what I read in the class newsletter, at least."

"I'm a psychologist, yeah. And you're in emergency medicine? I didn't know that was an interest of yours."

"It wasn't back when. I was convinced I'd make it as a country music singer, but after a single year playing low-rent music in some of the roughest bars, I decided it wasn't the gig for me." The grin he gave her was wry. "EMT was easy enough to get into. Seemed like I was the first on scene a lotta times, so I learned on my feet, so to speak. Got that certificate, and then I've added to the credentials through the years. I could work in an ER, but riding the bus fits me better."

"How'd you wind up here?" It could have meant in her house or on the coast, and Mya didn't care which way he took his answer. She just wanted to hear his voice. Slow and still tinged with a faint drawl, the tone of it was as comfortable as a warm blanket.

"After I got my little brother through school, there wasn't much left for me in the hometown. All my buddies had left, and my best friend had been gone for years. That's you, if you didn't remember." His lips shifted into a pink pout, then slid easily into another grin. "Riley joined the military. He went into the Navy, and it's been good for him. Gave him the structure he'd been lacking."

Mya remembered the Martinez house as a place of refuge, but she knew the surface could be very different from reality. *Take my own childhood home as an example.*

"Your mom?" She didn't need to ask about his dad. Mr. Martinez had died their freshman year.

"She passed a couple years ago." Kade didn't hide the grief that settled on his features, brow pulling together into a dark frown, mouth downturned with the pain. "Was a blessing when she went."

"Doesn't change how much it hurts, though." Mya closed her eyes. "Daddy's been gone for years, and Mom only lasted a few months past that. She'd been hurting so long, I couldn't hold her responsible when she decided to end things."

"God, Mya. I didn't know that was how it went down." His palm settled on her belly, a warm weight that reassured her. "I'm so sorry about your mom. That's a hard thing to live through."

"Thanks. I've come to understand. Like I said, it doesn't change how much it still has the power to hurt, though." Blowing out a breath made her flinch, and she lifted her head, staring down her body. She thought the bruising might look worse than it had only half an hour ago, and she now saw the stripe of blue across her lower belly. "This is all from the seat belt, right?"

"Yeah, and your head is from first smacking the inside of the car and then falling from nearly a meter up when you unbuckled the belt. That wasn't the smartest thing to do, FYI. We were right there when I saw you fall. Another ten seconds, and we'd have been able to get you out in a way that wouldn't have caused additional pain."

"Suffering is the human condition." Mya scrunched up her face, pleased when that didn't do anything other than make her head pound an extra beat. "Least my face survived the accident."

"That's nothing but luck and more luck. You had enough glass on your face to blind you if it had gotten into your eyes." Kade's lips flattened again, turning white. "Then walking yourself out of the car? I was right there, Mya. I could have helped you."

"I recognized your voice." She hadn't meant to tell him that. It was a sideways admission that his teenage self still had a hold on her. "I heard you talking and just knew I'd be okay."

Kade's eyes closed, face shifting as if something pained him. "Remember what we told each other in sixth grade? Still true." His lids flew open, and he stared at her fiercely. "I will always be there for you, Mya. Then. Now. Another ten years down the road? Still true."

"I still have the scar." She tried to change the direction of their conversation in an attempt to defuse the emotion that had broken through. Distractedly, she itched the skin of her palm. "Might not have been the best idea, rubbing dirt into the wounds."

"It was what my dad always said. 'Rub a little dirt on it. You'll be fine.' Made perfect sense to me at the time." The intensity of his expression eased as he followed the shift she'd introduced. "I'm glad I was the one on the call last night. So glad."

"How did I not wind up in the hospital? You never really said, and I honestly don't remember much past getting out of the car and seeing you, then the ambulance. It's like I blacked out, but I know I didn't." Mya let her fingers explore the boundaries of the bruising on her chest, flexing her fingers and forearms. "Everything's sore."

"You wouldn't go to the hospital. Nothing I could say would change your mind. Then you pointed down the street and showed us your house. Said you'd be okay, could walk home, and you were fine." His facial features tightened, jaw jutting as his Adam's apple bobbed down and up. "I couldn't make you ride the bus, but I damn sure wasn't about to let you stay here alone. We were at the end of shift, so I told my partner I'd owe him one if he'd do the rig transfer without me. By that time, he knew we were old friends. Fortunately, he agreed with only a little ribbing."

"And so you came home with me? To watch over me?" Heat prickled the backs of Mya's eyes, and she blinked fast, trying to dissuade salty tears from welling up. "That's so … Kade. Just so you." She gripped his hand, holding tightly. "Thank you."

Kade's mouth opened, but before he could respond, a buzzing rattled from the nightstand on his side of the bed. Mya watched as he closed his eyes, rolling to his back and away as he released her hand. He lifted the phone to his ear and grunted. A change came over his face, lines hardening more than before.

"What?" He barked the question, and she could faintly hear the sound of a man's voice through the phone's speaker. "You're kidding me? Reapers?" That wasn't as harshly spoken, but still with a tone of displeasure. "Yeah, hold him there. I'll be there in—Shit, I don't have my ride or my colors, brother. I'll let you know my ETA once I'm on the bike. Don't let him leave." More speaking from the other party on the call, and Kade grunted. "Whatever it takes," he said in response, then disconnected the call.

"Mya, I've gotta go." He rolled back to face her, pushing up on an elbow to look down, his face hovering over hers. "There's a thing—"

Her phone rang from the other nightstand, and Mya held up a finger as she slowly wriggled onto her side to reach the device. The screen showed it was from her answering service, which meant it was an emergency. She connected the call.

"Hello, Dr. Taylor here." Mya was glad to find her most professional voice came out sounding normal. The mattress shifted, and she glanced back to see Kade on his feet beside the bed, already bent to grab something from the floor.

"Sorry to bother you, Dr. Taylor, but one of your patients has been hospitalized. They're asking for a phone consult ASAP." The woman from the service rattled off a number, and Mya's phone buzzed with an incoming text. "I've sent it to your phone to make it easier, Doctor."

"Thank you. I'll give them a call right now." Mya hesitated, then sighed. Kade was pulling on his jeans, giving her a frown that prompted her next words. She admitted, "I was in a car accident last night, so let's route any additional calls to the other Dr. Taylor, okay?"

"Oh my gosh, are you okay? Do you need anything?" The woman's voice was filled with worry. "I'm so sorry I had to call. Do you want Dr. Taylor to take this consult instead?"

"No, it's okay. I can answer a few questions from the attending. Thank you again. You're too sweet."

The call disconnected, and Mya looked at the text, recognizing the patient's name as well as the number. He'd gone to Central, which had a good psychiatric unit, so that was a plus for her patient.

"So you've got work?" Kade's voice came from the foot of the bed, and Mya looked to see him already dressed in khaki pants and tugging on worn but comfortable-looking boots. "You aren't going to try to drive anywhere, are you?"

"No, not until my head stops hurting so much. I'll do this one consult and then take the rest of the weekend off. My Friday night will simply extend through the next couple of days."

He studied her for a moment, mouth opening and closing twice. Finally, he asked, "The other Dr. Taylor?"

Mya smiled. "Coincidence. We both work at the clinic, so the service has to make sure they call the right one. It can be confusing sometimes. He's a good guy." She paused, then pointed at the dresser where her purse lay. "My keys are in there. You can use my car if you want. Just leave me your phone number so we can connect to transfer it back."

Kade grinned, the smile so wide and bright it took her back a couple of decades to the boy who'd featured in all her dreams. "My digits are already in your phone, and I texted myself, so I've got yours too. I wasn't about to let you get away again."

"Let me get away?" Mya slowly sat up, reaching for the sheet kicked to the bottom of the bed. She lay back, relaxing her protesting muscles as the fabric drifted over her.

"You know." Kade's face had turned closed off again, the taut muscles along his jaw telling her he was done talking about whatever he'd meant. "I'll have your car back today.

Thanks for the offer. It's seriously going to save me some time."

"I'll see you later?" Mya curled up on her side, finding a position that hurt the least. "Until then, I'll take it easy. No need to coach me."

"Hold on." He turned and strode out the door. She heard sounds from the farthest reaches of her bungalow, a cabinet door opening, then a couple minutes later, a clatter of pottery. An additional few minutes later, he reappeared in the doorway with a glass, a small plate, and a bottle of generic painkillers. Arranging them on the nightstand, he pointed. "Water, a piece of toast with a little butter, and stuff for your head." Kade appeared to hesitate, staring down at her, then he bent from the waist, and Mya felt the lightest brush of his lips against her temple. "See you soon, Mya."

"See you."

Chapter Two

Mya tested the limits of her still-angry ribs with a big breath, smiling to herself when the movement felt better than it had for days. She hadn't had to reschedule any of her clinic appointments, but it had been a near thing in those first days post-accident. Her headache was still hanging around, not surprising given the mild concussion gained when she'd fallen to the top of the car. Even that was easing day by day, and she expected it to be gone within the next couple of days.

She'd spent the time before Kade returned her car on the phone with Karen for two hours. Her friend had to be talked off the ledge when she realized the crash that had been on the news was their rideshare. Only after promising to come over for dinner the next day had Mya been able to close out the call. She smiled at the memory.

Good friends are a blessing, even if they're a little bossy.

When Kade had come back, he'd been standoffish and brusque, barely crossing the threshold and only softening his stance when she'd opened her arms for a goodbye hug. A battered pickup had been idling at the curb, and she'd watched Kade stride down the walk and swing into the passenger side of the cab. The vehicle had pulled away smoothly, and her last sight of Kade had been the back of one tattooed hand raised in goodbye.

There'd been nothing since, which shouldn't be surprising given they were grown adults with lives that had been lived separately for years, but Mya kept trying to push away the persistent compulsion to evaluate her emotions. So what if she was feeling a little hurt? They'd gone decades without talking. Now that each knew the other was near, a brief break in the reconnection wasn't abnormal.

He's got his own life, silly woman. Probably has a boyfriend or maybe a...partner.

She didn't remember a band on his finger, but given he'd been working, that really didn't tell her anything. And the feelings stirred by the thought of Kade having a significant other were something else she was going to ignore.

Movement on the bookshelf opposite where she sat caught her eye as the display for a discretely placed security camera showed a tall woman walking down the hallway leading to the offices. Standing from her comfortable armchair, she smoothed down the back of her slacks and waited for the chime of the office entrance alarm to ring before striding to the door. This next client was punctual to a fault, and Mya always felt she could set a watch to the arrival.

"Evan, hello," she said, pulling the door open. "Come in."

"I'm early, I know," the woman said apologetically.

"It's never a problem." She stepped back and allowed the woman to pick a seat without prompting. As usual, the least comfortable chair was her selection.

"How have the past couple of weeks been?" Angling the armchair to give her a view of her client, Mya smiled softly. "When we last spoke, you had a couple of goals in mind. Why don't you tell me how those have gone?"

The next forty-five minutes passed quickly, and they closed out the session on a good note, with Evan leaving holding notes Mya had passed over about her goals. Not every client needed a to-do list, but if it was what would help them move past their own insecurities, Mya would use any tool to give them success. Success was what was needed to build on, after all.

Closing the door behind Evan, Mya checked the clock on the wall. Nearly seven, and time to pack up for home. Ten minutes later, she'd set the clinic's alarm and exited to the parking garage. She slowed her pace when she saw someone leaning against her car, only regaining speed once she recognized Kade.

"Hey," she offered, coming to a stop a few feet away. "Imagine running into you here."

"Hey," he responded softly, shifting to stand upright. "Wondered if you were going home soon. Thought maybe I could talk you into dinner."

"With you?" The instant the words were out of her mouth, Mya cringed. "Sorry, that was thoughtless. I just … how did you know where my office was?"

"Yes, with me." He smirked, one corner of his mouth curling up slightly. "And you're listed on the interwebs. Never let it be said I can't operate a search engine."

"Oh. Yeah, that makes sense." Mya swallowed hard, making an instant decision. "Dinner sounds good. Want me to follow you somewhere, or…"

When she trailed off, his smirk transformed into a wide smile. "Or something, yeah. Thought you could ride with me. If you aren't put off someone else's driving, that is?"

Gaze glued to his smile, focused on attractive lines framing his mouth that advertised how often his face wore that expression, all Mya could do was nod.

"I'm over here." He angled his chin over her shoulder, and she turned to see a pickup parked nearby. It was different from the one that had picked him up from her house. "My ride isn't new, but it's reliable."

"Reliable is good," she agreed. "Let me just put my stuff in the trunk."

Before she could do more than click the button on her fob, he'd taken her bags and tucked them inside the opened trunk, looking up at her. "You won't need your purse, unless you feel naked without it?"

"Let me get my phone." Most restaurants accepted digital wallet payments, so even without her purse, she'd be okay.

"Here you go." He handed her back the small shoulder bag, and she grabbed her phone out.

Walking to the truck, she felt the briefest brush of heat against the small of her back, a guiding touch of his hand. That was a gesture she associated with a lover, and Mya straightened, moving away from Kade slightly. The heat dropped away as he reached for the door handle, dragging it open for her. He waited there for her to climb awkwardly into the taller-than-expected vehicle, then closed it as she settled into the seat and smoothed her pants legs. Her phone made an uncomfortable bulge in the tiny pocket, and she couldn't remember why she'd insisted on bringing it but not her purse.

"You sure you're good with this?" Kade was seated in the driver's seat, arm farthest away from her dangling from the wrist propped on the steering wheel. His other hand was spread over the back of her seat, fingers grazing gently and rhythmically against the hot skin of her neck. "Riding with me?"

"Yes." She shook her head. "I mean, of course. You were the teacher's pet of driver's ed, after all."

Kade snorted and twisted to face forwards. She immediately missed the heat from his touch and scolded herself.

We're just friends. Reconnecting doesn't mean changing. He's gay, remember?

The engine roared to life, startling her so she jumped in place. Soft country music played over the radio, and she laughed quietly at that additional reminder of the boy she'd grown up with.

"You always loved country." Mya pulled her seat belt into place, listening for the click. She tested it a couple of times, yanking discreetly against the lock, ensuring it was secure. She'd been doing the same thing while driving to work too. The therapist in her knew it was a way to ensure another good outcome in case of a wreck, even while she understood it was unlikely that she'd be involved in another accident. Maybe ever, but probabilities had the likelihood of any additional accidents happening way beyond when she'd have forgotten to check the belt again.

"Yup. Still do. What do you listen to? Disastrous indie alt stuff?" He was smiling as he looked over his shoulder, backing out of the parking space. She'd caught his gaze as it glanced over her hands and knew he'd noticed her obsessive behavior.

"Worse." She waited a beat for dramatic effect. "Cool jazz, mostly."

"Oh, no! The horror!" The grin on his lips belied his distressed tone. "What have you done with my Mya?"

"Grown out of who I was, mostly." She answered him honestly. It had always been that way between them, at least until the very end when she'd kept a secret so big it felt like it would smother her. "Change is inevitable for some of us."

"Not me. I'm still a simple country boy at heart. Good music, cheap beer, winding roads, and my bike." He patted a folded piece of leather on the console between them. "Riding with my brothers is life, man."

"Brothers?" She angled herself against the door to watch him as he drove. His expression was relaxed, chin up confidently, and his eyes were bright with excitement of some kind. The leather seemed to be a garment, with an insignia sewed into place on the back panel.

"Yeah, in the club. Closer than blood, most of us. We do nearly everything together." He snorted a soft laugh. "I caught shit earlier when I showed up at the clubhouse in the truck instead of on the bike. Told everyone I had a classy lady to take to dinner and didn't want to arrive all bug splattered."

"Does that really happen? The bugs?" Mya tried to adjust her memories and understanding of Kade to take in this new knowledge. "And you're in a motorcycle club?" She was careful to use the same terms he had to describe this thing he felt so passionate about. "That's not something I'd have expected. Aren't you worried about wrecking?"

"Yeah, the bugs are a real thing. Some months are worse than others, as you'd expect." His turn indicator blinked as he took the next left. "And yeah, I'm in a club. I'm the president." He paused, and she noted the way his facial features sharpened, tension pulling the muscles taut. "Is that a problem, Doctor?"

"What?" Mya sputtered, then waved a hand at him. "No, of course not. It's just new info. Give a gal a minute to process, would ya?" When some of the tension left his face, she laughed softly. "You like these people you're in the club with, then? That's good. A connection like that is stronger than just friends, isn't it?"

"Yeah. Like I said, closer than blood. They're my found family. I'd do anything to protect every one of them." The tension was entirely gone now, a smile again playing along his lips. "Took me a while to get over my own attitude. Wasn't sure it was something I wanted, but taking the bike out alone isn't as much fun, so I hung around them for some group rides. Got to know a few of them, then a few more." He laughed, chin rising with the burst of humor. "Found out later that's how they hook a guy they think would be a good member. Draw them in with a bunch of fun times, and then throw a patch on their back soon as they'll accept it." He shook his head, apparently at a memory. "Good guys. I'm proud of them."

"How long have you been in the club? Is it a name I'd know?" From news stories, she meant, hoping he'd say no.

"About five years now." Kade's head shook back and forth. "And no, not likely you'd know the name, unless you saw a report on a charity run we'd done. The Eusebeia's Pets MC aren't into shit that'd catch big news. We keep our shit on lockdown."

"What was the name again?" She thought she'd caught it, but wasn't certain.

"Eusebeia's Pets. It's Greek—"

She interrupted him. "Greek for piety, right?"

"Mosty right." He glanced her way. "We lean towards the loyalty and duty part of the definition."

"That's good, right? I love the meaning and intent behind the name." She dragged through her memories but came up blank with any associations for the club. "I don't think I've ever heard of them, sorry. I guess not everything is like it's portrayed on TV."

Another laugh burst from him, this one bitter. The ugly sound bounced around the cab of the truck for a second, and she saw his shoulders tighten. "Nope. TV gets a lotta shit wrong. Not everything, but a lot. We don't have any feuds, but we do have friction with another club. They're new to town, but you might see them on the news. Waterfront Reapers." He said the name like spitting out something disgusting. "Nothing to worry about." He paused, changing lanes, and Mya found herself watching the surrounding traffic intently. Kade pulled her attention back to him with a soft "Hey."

"Hmmm?"

"I'm a good driver, Mya. Promise." He dropped the hand closest to her to the console, placing it palm up invitingly. "You're safe with me. Always."

Mya reached for his hand, slipping her fingers between his much bigger ones, pulling in the first easy breath she'd taken since they'd started the trip. He gave her a squeeze, and she returned the gesture, a glance at his face showing the smile that broke over his lips.

"I know. And I'm not nervous, at least not on purpose. It's just so recent." She pulled in another huge breath, liking the stretch as her ribs expanded. "Logically I understand. Trust me, I've analyzed the accident from a thousand different directions but haven't come up with a way I could have changed the outcome."

"So you're not doing the coulda, woulda, shoulda, at least."

She smiled at his frown. *Just like Kade, trying to take care of everyone.*

"Nope. And I'm aware of the various coping mechanisms I've adopted. Currently everything falls within normal parameters for someone dealing with the aftermath of an out-of-control situation like that."

His amused snort brought her up short.

"What?"

"You sound like a psychologist."

"Well, I am one. As you should know from your search engine mastery. Don't act all surprised." His fingers tightened on her hand again, and she laughed. "No, I get it. Who'd have thought that a straight-A student would want so much more schooling? But brain games are what I do. If it can be analyzed, I'm your gal."

He gave a sharp nod. "You are."

Turning off the main road, Kade steered the truck down a packed dirt road. The trees closed in on both sides of the track, and Mya searched through the brush for signs of a business.

"Where are we? This is a part of town I'm not familiar with." If it had been anyone other than Kade, she'd have been seriously afraid right about now, and even knowing him as well as she did, there was a tiny frisson of fear dancing up her spine. "You didn't say where we were going."

"Best place around for grilled steaks and baked potatoes." Easy and relaxed, Kade swung his head to glance at her. "I'd planned on taking you to a fancy restaurant, but then we got to talking, and muscle memory took over. Good thing I've got a stocked fridge."

Startled, Mya looked out the windows again, still seeing nothing more than forest crowding each side of the narrow track. "We're going to your house?"

"Seems fair, seeing as I know where you live." He nodded at her lap. "Makes it so you can add the map pin to my contact too. You're welcome here anytime, Mya. Mi casa es su casa."

Picking up her phone, she did as he suggested, struggling a bit to do it one-handed, but she found herself unwilling to release her hold on his hand. That connection made every breath easier and quieted her mind. Having a pin on the map for his house settled her nerves even more.

Of course it will. He's important. He was a big part of younger me and helped forge me into who I am today. Still, glad I brought the phone after all.

"Okay. Got it." She laughed softly, then fell silent when his home came into view.

A large log cabin sat in a huge clearing, trees and underbrush cut back well away from the structure. More than ample lighting came from two tall security lights that snapped to brightness as the truck crawled closer to the building. The dirt drive turned to pavement as it widened, filling the space in front of an attached garage. Faintly, she could make out the sound of barking, seeming to come from inside the house. The noise grew in volume suddenly, and three canines swept around the far corner of the building, quickly arrowing straight for the driver door of the now-parked truck.

"Promise my dogs won't hurt you. The big one is Bo, smaller is Daisy, and the middle furry thang is Luke." He opened his door. "Sit tight. I'll come around and introduce you."

Mya was bemused as she tried to think of why the names sounded familiar, and just before Kade opened her door, the memory came into focus. She was holding her side laughing when he swung the door wide, fumbling to unfasten her seat belt as she patted the air.

"Give—" Mya pulled in a hard breath, throwing her head back as the laughter came back in full force. "Give me a minute." Twisting in the seat, she carefully angled her body out of the vehicle, conscious he reached for her waist to steady her, but she was more focused on the source of her amusement. "Oh God, Kade. That's priceless."

"What?" He looked entirely bemused, his gaze flicking across her face as he took in her laughter. "What's so funny? Share?"

"You named your dogs Bo, Luke, and Daisy. Do you have a Rosco, too?" When his brows knit in a frown, she burst into renewed amusement. "Oh my God. You do! The Hazzard gang rides again."

Realization spread across his face, features softening into a smile. "Yeah, that's where they came from." He patted the top of the truck, wrapping his other hand around hers to pull her away from the vehicle. "And yes, this is the General."

"That was your favorite show. You'd catch it on the oldies channel and watch every episode you could."

"Simpler times." Attention on the dogs at his feet, Kade dropped his other hand to rest on the head of the largest one. "Bo, this is Mya. She's ours, got it? Ours. Guard."

The dog immediately grew attentive and rose to his feet to circle Mya, sniffing as he went.

"What kind of dog is he?" She gestured towards the other ones. "They're all the same breed, right?"

"Yeah, they're from the same litter. Vet thinks they're mostly King Shepherds mixed with a little of this and that. They're great loyal companions and unfalteringly fierce." Bo completed his circuit and returned to sit with the others. He stared up at Mya, eyes dialed in on her face. "He'll keep you safe now."

"What? Just from you telling him that?"

"Yeah. Not only is it in his blood, but I've been rigorous with their training. Daisy, Luke, this is Mya. She's ours." The other two dogs immediately rose to their feet and followed the same behavior Bo had. "Now you're triple safe."

"I don't know what I need to be safe from out here." She gestured around the clearing. "But thanks. It's been a while since someone wanted to ensure my safety." Glancing up at Kade, she asked, "Can I pet them, or is it like a service dog, and they're working now?"

"Nah, you can pet them all you want. Just be firm with an 'off' command if they happen to try and jump up. Luke gets all amped up sometimes. I take them on a drive sometimes and Bo will be all kinds of chill, but when I try to take Luke, he's a different beast."

Movement at the corner of the house caught Mya's attention, and she looked over to see a large bloodhound waddling his way through the yard. His ears nearly dragged the ground, and as he came closer, she could make out the mass of wrinkles on his face. His nose was up and sweeping side to side slightly, and the dog didn't stop his forward momentum until he was only inches away from Mya's legs.

"And this is Rosco, of course." She smiled down at the dog, who'd perked up at the sound of his name. She squatted and stroked down his ears, rubbing the tips lightly. Roscoe let out a loud groan and took a step closer so he could rest his chin on her bent leg. "Oh, you're a treasure."

Mya looked up to find Kade smiling down at her, an expression flitting over his face that she thought looked a lot like longing. Gazes locked, she reached out a hand, and he caught at her fingers, dropping to a knee next to her.

"Bo." His voice croaked. "Come get some lovin', boy."

Instantly, Mya's other side was enveloped in furry heat as the dog plastered himself to her ribs, his head sneaking underneath her arm and lifting her hand away from Rosco's ears.

With a grin at Kade, she detached from his hold and proceeded to make all four dogs as happy as she could, fingers finding itchy spots that drew groans and whines from them in turn. Mya wasn't sure how long they stayed that way, but it wasn't until her head gave a ragged pound that she realized it had been a while.

Pushing off the ground, she tried to ignore the aches in her knees and back, but Kade must have recognized her struggle because, midmovement, his arm circled her waist, and he pulled her effortlessly the rest of the way to her feet.

"Thanks," she murmured, brushing her palms together as she looked around the clearing again. Darkness had fallen in earnest, and all she could see were swaying shadows in the dimness. "You're so remote out here. Do you worry about being so far from civilization?"

"Nah. I like it. The quiet is soothing. Privacy doesn't suck either." He took her hands in his, brushing away imaginary dirt and dog hair. "Come inside. I can't wait for you to see where I live."

"How often do you get guests way out here?" She followed his lead, and when he linked their fingers together, she allowed herself to be pulled along in his wake.

"More often than you'd think. My brothers spend a bit of time here. I've got a good garage setup, so we'll bring their rides out to do oil changes or work on problems." He waved a hand to the side where the garage was attached to the end of the house. "We cook outside, and usually someone's old lady will bring a grocery getter with coolers of beer."

"Old lady?" He hadn't said the words derisively but with respect, so she used the same tenor to ask for clarification.

"Their partner. He's the lady's old man, and she's his old lady. Old lady is a title worn with pride, because it doesn't just show a sense of possession, but implies exclusiveness." Kade tossed the response out over his shoulder, not seeming to take offense, for which Mya was glad. "And before you ask, no, I've never had an old anything."

Even though Kade couldn't see the movement, Mya shook her head. "I wasn't going to ask." There was a nudge against her thigh, and she looked down to see Bo striding beside her. "Bo's taking his job seriously."

"He should" was Kade's only response, and she giggled lightly. "What? I told him he had work to do, so he's doing it. My dogs enjoy having a purpose."

"They're like people in that way."

Kade paused at the door and thumbed in a code on a nearby keypad. The latch popped free, and he pushed the door wide, tugging Mya inside behind him. He didn't stop to close it, and Mya missed her chance to swing it shut. Then she saw why Kade didn't worry about it. Luke stopped beside the door and, once the other three dogs had come inside, nudged it with his nose until it clicked back into place.

"You've got your own automatic door closer. That's pretty cool."

"That's one I can't take credit for. He started that all on his own." Kade glanced over his shoulder at Mya, a bemused look pulling his brows high. "They're ridiculously smart."

"Their intelligence is evident."

"Forty-five one zero eight."

"I'm sorry?" She looked up to find his gaze fixed on her. "I missed something."

"Forty-five one zero eight. Code to that door, also works on the rest of the doors, and the toolboxes you haven't yet seen. Forty-five one zero eight."

"Your address." The information leapt into her mind. "That was your address, back home."

"Yeah." He shrugged. "Easy to remember."

That felt too casual, but she couldn't put her finger on why.

Once they reached the kitchen, Kade dropped her hand and immediately turned to the refrigerator, working behind the opened door to pull out a variety of food options. They included the promised steak and potatoes, and she started nosing around his cabinets. He had salad fixings, so she found a big bowl and got busy washing things at the sink.

"Hey." His hand landed on her hip, tugging slightly. "You don't have to do that. I didn't bring you out here to feed me. I'm the chef tonight."

"I can sous chef like a boss," she teased, tossing him a grin over her shoulder. "I figured the meat should be your territory, but persnickety stuff like salad I can help with."

Kade swayed closer, and Mya stilled. When his lips touched her temple, she let out a shaky breath.

"You're still my best friend, Mya." He pulled back, his gaze flicking back and forth to look at her eyes. "Just finish up

the washing and come keep me company outside, yeah?"
His hand gave her hip a squeeze, and she nodded.

As he walked away, carrying a pan holding the food for the grill, Luke and Daisy followed him, while Bo remained only a few feet away from Mya. Rosco was nowhere to be seen, and she smiled at the mental image of him sprawled out snoring in a dog bed somewhere.

Mya shook herself and turned back to the sink, hands moving automatically as she worked with the head of lettuce, peppers, radishes, and tomatoes, ensuring everything was clean and draining before she walked away.

Chapter Three

Mya

Their evening together had turned into an overnight, with Mya bedding down in one of Kade's guest rooms. She'd woken the next morning with an insistent Bo tugging the covers off, his unrelenting movements goading her out of bed.

She smiled now as she remembered catching sight of Kade standing in the kitchen, casually leaning a hip against the countertop as he lifted a mug of coffee to his lips, unable to hide his grin. Without asking, she'd known he'd sent the dog in to wake her.

Now, three days later, seated at her laptop making notes from her day's patients, Mya glanced at her phone. It had remained persistently quiet, at least regarding Kade.

With a sigh at herself, she grabbed it and thumbed open the text app, going to the short string with Kade.

*Wanna hang out tonight? Movie at my place, maybe?

Tapping the Send button with more force than necessary, she grumbled, "There. I texted him. Are you happy now?"

"Depends. Should I be happy?" Lawrence Taylor—the clinic's other Dr. Taylor—stood in the open doorway, smiling at her.

"You're annoying." She crumpled up a tiny piece of note paper and tossed it at him. They both laughed when it barely cleared the other side of her desk. "Pick that up, would you?"

He stepped into the room and stooped to grab the paper, reaching around the side of the desk to toss it into the trash can. "Why am I annoying today?"

She eyed him as he settled into one of the chairs facing her. "That. That's why you're annoying today. Did I invite you in?"

Their banter was as comfortable as ever. The two of them had become friends during her residency, and while it had never been more—mostly since she had still been pining over Kade, and Law was gay as the day was long—the friendship had deepened and been one of the main reasons she'd accepted the offer to practice at this clinic.

"I just had a feeling you needed me." He steepled his fingers in front of his lips. "Would this annoyance have anything to do with the fact I'm not the person you'd like to see?"

Before she could answer him, her phone buzzed loudly against the desktop, and then again, a couple more times in rapid succession. Mya warred with herself for only a moment before grabbing it eagerly and looking at the screen.

*Damn. Can't.

*Sorry. I've been looped into something here.

*Unless you wouldn't mind changing plans?

*Ever been on a bike?

Mya quickly typed out her response, holding her breath as she sent it.

*Never. But I'm game. What do I need to wear?

Kade's return text was fast.

*Protective boots if you have them. Something sturdy at least. Jeans and a jacket. The wind gets chilly. I'll snag a helmet for you. Pick you up at home in 30?

Mya mentally ran through her wardrobe selections and sighed with relief. Her hiking boots would do, and since even here on the West Coast it got cold in the winter, she had a plethora of jackets.

*Sounds great. I can't wait. You'll teach me what I need to know, right?

She smiled as his response came back just as fast.

*You betcha. I'll take care with you.

Take care with me, not of me.

*See you soon.

"You've completely forgotten I'm here, haven't you?" Law's dry laugh brought her back to herself with a start. "Don't answer. I can see it in your face. Hot date, huh? That's why you were texting and glad of it?"

"It's Kade." She kept her face as impassive as possible, then broke, sharing a wide smile with him. "I'm going on a ride on his bike."

Lawrence knew all about Kade. Both past-Kade, the lost love of her life, and present-Kade, her found-again friend. She'd spent hours self-analyzing in discussion with Law, even as he'd picked apart his own past, both of them wrapped up in small-town challenges.

"Go get him, girlie." Law stood and clapped his hands, then made a shooing motion at her. "Get out of here, Mya. You have places to be. Charting can wait until Monday."

"It really can." She saved the patient notes she'd been working on, then efficiently closed out all the programs, setting the computer so it would back up, and then automatically shut down. "I've got a ride to ready for."

"Be safe, be smart, and above all—" Law leaned forward slightly as he finished. "—be hella brave."

"I will." She pulled in a deep breath. "I haven't asked him anything about what really happened with us back home yet. We've just covered the bare basics. But unlike way back when we were in high school, the vibes he's giving me now aren't mixed at all. Unless I'm reading him wrong."

"Girl, you haven't gone to school half your life to get things like this wrong. With the training we both have, it's really best to trust our guts. What is your belly telling you about Kade?" One corner of his mouth tipped up as if he already knew her answer.

"That he missed me. That maybe missing me woke him up to other possibilities." She shook her head. "But he took the football guy to the prom, Law."

"And bisexuality is a thing, Mya." Law mock glared at her. "As is gay, straight, and every other letter on the rainbow. Don't erase bi-ness. That's not a good look for anyone."

"But I don't know if he's bi."

"And you don't know that he's gay, either. Woman, we've talked about this a hundred times. As a teen, you assumed sexuality because of behavior, without asking for the facts. You know better methods now, and I vote you get the information straight from the horse's mouth, honey. Who, what, where, when, and why, just like we both learned long ago. Just the facts, ma'am."

"I know. But—"

"But nothing. Ask him. What's the worst? Isn't that what we tell our patients to do? Use your words, Mya. It's the only way you'll know the truth. And now go on. Get outta here. You're gonna be late."

Law ushered her out of the room, clicking the door shut behind them. He grabbed his case from his office, closing that door as well, then setting the alarm as they exited. Together, they walked down to where their cars were parked in side-by-side reserved spaces. When Law placed his hand on her arm, she stopped and looked up at him.

"Be safe, be smart—"

"And be brave," she finished for him. "I will." Covering his hand with her own, she grinned. "You're making me late, Law."

"Heaven forbid," he exclaimed, spinning away. "I can't wait to hear every detail, Dr. Taylor."

"I'm not the kind of girl to kiss and tell, Dr. Taylor, but you'll be my first call either way."

"I can conference Karen in. No need to hurt the poor girl's feelings. We're both your besties, I know."

Mya was still laughing as she buckled her seat belt and started the car. She caught a glimpse of herself in the rearview mirror and paused, staring at the sparkling eyes and upturned lips that faced her.

"I remember you," she said softly, then threw the car into Reverse and checked her mirrors before backing out of her spot.

Twenty-five minutes later, Mya was nervously standing at the end of the sidewalk in front of her house. Shifting her weight from foot to foot, she froze in place as soon as she heard the rumble of motorcycle pipes in the distance. The roar gradually grew louder, and Mya turned to face the direction she intuited Kade would come from. A moment later, she found out why the noise was so loud when not one, but four bikes swept around the corner at the end of the block. They were in an obvious formation, and she recognized Kade riding at the front of the staggered line configuration.

He angled towards the curb, the other bikes spreading out and coming into a single line behind him. Focused on Kade's face, she didn't pay attention to the other men. Behind the clear windscreen on his helmet, she could see his wide smile aimed directly at her. Mya gave him a little wave low, then mentally rolled her eyes at how dorky she was acting.

Shaking off her nerves, Mya strode to where Kade sat astride his idling bike.

"Hi." She spun in a tidy circle. "Is this okay?"

"You look great, Mya. That's perfect. Let's get the helmet on, and I'll show you how to ride behind me." He made a gesture, then reached for the handlebars of his bike. The sound cut off suddenly, and Mya looked up as one of the other men approached. "That's Torch. His old lady keeps a helmet at the clubhouse, so we're gonna use that today."

"Hey," Torch said, handing Mya the helmet. "Glad you're gonna be K-Man's backpack today." He turned and walked away, already talking to one of the other men.

"K-Man?" She studied the helmet for a moment before settling it on her head. Kade reached up and fastened the strap underneath her chin, adjusting the fit, then patted the top of her head.

"He's an idiot, but we love him." The smile Kade wore was muted but affectionate. "I think you're set, honey." He pointed down to the side of the bike. "Put your foot on that little peg and swing your leg over to get on behind me. Find the peg on the other side, then slide up close and hold on to my belt or around my waist."

"Okay." She rested a hand on the seat and leaned slightly to look down the other side, where she saw a matching footrest. "Got it." Once she had both feet firmly on what he'd called a peg, she gripped his belt on either side. "Like this?"

Warmth wrapped around each of her calves, Kade's hands curling and gripping. Then he tugged her knees out and up, and Mya held her breath as she slid across the supple leather of the motorcycle seat until she was wrapped directly around Kade's hips.

"No, more like this." His response was belated but threaded through with humor.

"Got it," she told him, resettling her feet on the pegs. "And my hands?"

"Go ahead and wrap 'em around me, honey. Hang on tight. Once we're underway, just move with me. This is an easy run, but don't worry. I'll take care."

Mya leaned against his back and slid her hands around his waist, letting them overlap across his stomach. The bike rumbled to life underneath them, and Mya's arms tightened in response, gripping tighter.

Kade turned his head slightly, and she could see the open-mouthed grin he wore. "Ready?" He called the question over his shoulder while making a gesture with his right hand. Mya nodded, and he made another gesture. Facing front, she saw him check his mirrors and did the same, seeing a thumbs-up from each man behind them.

The bike moved away from the curb slowly at first but picked up speed quickly.

It didn't take long for Mya to appreciate Kade's advice of wearing jeans and a jacket, because the wind whipping past would have been chilling otherwise. She realized Kade's body blocked most of the wind, and she focused on staying tight against his back.

A couple of miles into the ride, the four of them met up with a much larger group. Kade maneuvered into a spot at the end of the existing line, the other riders falling into place beside and behind him. Mya peered forward over his shoulder and saw the double line of motorcycles stretched out quite a distance. There were probably forty or fifty bikes in total.

"Where are we going?" Mya shouted her question, unsure how loud she needed to be for Kade to hear her.

"It's a multiple club charity run, so there are quite a few stops. The first one should be in about twenty minutes." Kade took his left hand off the handlebar, and his palm curled around her calf. He gave her a squeeze that made her belly warm. *Nope. I'm ignoring that.* "How ya doin', honey?"

"I'm good." She tightened her grip on his waist, returning the squeeze.

"All right."

He didn't say anything else, which wasn't surprising with the difficulty in holding a conversation with the wind rushing past, but his hand stayed on her leg. Kade's palm slipped down and back up, the stroking motion firm and comforting.

At the final stop of the ride, which she'd found out was a fundraiser for a local family with a very sick child, Mya stretched her arms as Kade killed the bike's engine. Gripping his shoulder, she stood on the pegs and swung off to the left side of the bike. He'd explained that to her at the first stop, showing how it kept her away from the hot exhaust pipes running down the other side of the bike.

Kade keeled the bike to the side, the weight resting on the kickstand. He gave it a slight shake as he stood up, then turned to take her helmet off. Mya lifted her chin to allow him access to the strap, grinning at the studious expression on his face.

"Water or something harder?" He twisted to place the helmet on the ground next to his own. "This is the last stop. Once I check in and pay for my cards, we can stay or go." As he looked at her over his shoulder, she felt the weight of his gaze as he tracked down and back up her form. "Up to you."

"If we leave early, what do we do?" Mya pulled in a deep breath. "I've had such a good time. I hate for the evening to end."

"Didn't say anything about ending anything, Mya." Kade stood straight, facing her. The expression on his face smoothed, becoming more of a blank mask. His lips thinned, and she was thrust back to the night of the accident when she'd seen anger and pain on his face.

Pain. Because I hurt him. Law's face slipped through her thoughts, and she heard him again. *"Use your words."*

"I'd like to hang out again, if you're up for it." She glanced around at the milling crowd of people. "If your duties are fulfilled, maybe we could go somewhere a little more private?"

The smile unfolding across his face lit up the inside of her soul, spreading warmth through her. "Nothin' I'd like more, Mya. Give me half a minute, and I'll settle up inside." He reached out a hand and smoothed the hair on the side of her head, his fingers ghosting around the shell of her ear. "Back in a flash, honey."

Mya stood, watching him walk effortlessly across the parking lot. She grinned when he was stopped by half a dozen people on his way inside, each of them earning a back-thumping embrace from Kade. When he disappeared through the doorway into the building that bore a sign echoing the insignia on the back of his and his men's vests, she shuffled her feet, glancing around the group of people nearby.

"K-Man's a good one, lady."

Mya turned to find Torch standing next to her, facing the building as she'd been. "He really is."

At her agreement, the man grinned, his face transforming from a scowling visage to one that looked open and easy. "Glad to hear it. He's talked about nothing but his Mya for the past weeks. Gotta love our Prez, but it's turned into a broken record. All the why's and what's rollin' around in his head are keeping the rest of us up at night."

"What?" *His Mya?*

"Woman, watch when he comes back out. If you don't see it on his face, you gotta be blind. K-Man thinks the world of you. He's a good man."

"Blind?" She shook her head. "Not blind, but there's history here that you may not know about."

"I know more than you do," came his enigmatic response. "Now, here he comes. Watch."

Mya shifted her attention back to the doorway just as Kade walked through. His gaze immediately came to her, and the hopeful expression on his face was mixed with something else. Something she'd wanted to see for a long time. Hunger. *For me.*

"And there it is," Torch muttered, then tapped her shoulder with the palm of his hand. "Hopin' we get to see a lot more of you, Mya. Don't worry about the helmet. K-Man will get it back to me before my old lady needs it again. Be safe and trust him."

She vaguely heard Torch moving away, but Kade's prowl towards her captured nearly all her focus. One corner of his mouth tipped up as he stopped in front of her. "Ready to head out?"

All she could do was nod. Kade bent for the helmets and situated hers first. He climbed back on the bike, fitting his own helmet into place, then held up one hand, palm flattened invitingly. Mya gripped it for support, finding her place behind him, sliding up so they were pressed tightly together. Kade made an approving noise before he started the bike, his hand curling around her calf for a quick squeeze.

Then they were back on the road, alone this time, with no riders alongside or behind them to take up space. The bike was still loud, but she easily heard Kade's words when he asked, "My house or yours?"

"Yours" was her instant response. Her body heated as she remembered the hungry expression he'd worn as he looked at her. "Very much yours."

Chapter Four

Mya

Kade's hand on her back steered her around the house to the back door, and Mya laughed as she evaded the dogs winding between their legs. "They missed you."

"And you. Have a look at Bo there. He's all about gettin' your attention." Kade's hand slipped up her back, fingers curling around the nape of her neck. "He's gonna have to pony up in line, though. Hate to tell him."

"Oh, who else wants my attention?" Through the door, Mya turned to face him, careful not to dislodge his hand. She kept her tone light and teasing. "Anyone in particular?"

"Give you one guess." Kade's head angled down as his grip urged her to her toes. Their mouths met with a gentle slide, his sigh whispering against her lips. He straightened and pulled her close to his chest, arms wrapping around her shoulders. Mya rested her cheek against his chest, astonished that his heart was rocketing along just like hers. "God, Mya. You've no idea."

"I bet we both have questions. Should we clear those away, dissolve any doubts now?" Mya slipped her hands underneath his shirt, flattening her palms against the heated skin of his back.

He groaned at her touch, a shiver dancing through his muscles. His arms tightened slightly. "Yeah. We probably should." He didn't move, and neither did she. After a few moments, Kade laughed softly, and she felt the brush of his lips against her temple. "I don't wanna let you go, though."

"Couch snuggles, then?" She glanced over her shoulder. "It's less than fifteen feet away."

"Acceptable option." His arms squeezed and lifted, and suddenly, her feet were dangling, toes barely skimming the floor. Kade shuffled them to the couch, then sat with legs spread and settled her in the gap of his thighs, her body still held tight against his chest. "There." The single word came out on a gusty sigh that made her smile. "I like this."

She shifted into a more comfortable position, head against his shoulder so she could see his face. "Want me to go first?"

"Whatever makes you more comfortable, honey." He turned to look at her, and she saw the honesty there. "Works for me."

"Those last few months of school were so hard. Living with Daddy as he deteriorated was maddening, because he wouldn't see what was happening right in front of his face. What he was doing to us as a family." Mya swallowed. "Then the prom happened, and I lost my footing. After that, all I could think about was how to get away. Get out of that town and find a better place. A place that would fit me." She moved her gaze to track along the sharp edge of his throat, beard blurring the lines of his face. "I asked you to the prom because I wanted to tell you I loved you. Not as a best friend, but more."

"So you found an exit strategy." His tone carried no condemnation, no disappointment, and Mya blinked hard to keep sudden tears at bay. "Nothin' wrong with ensuring your own sanity."

"I should have talked to you." Blunt and to the point, she pushed through. "But I didn't have any idea you were gay. It hurt to think you'd held a secret like that, not believing you could tell me."

The bark of noise coming from him was so unexpected she startled, huddling closer as she realized what the sound was. Laughter.

Ignoring the interruption, she continued, "I'm not saying I didn't keep secrets too. Nobody knew about how bad Daddy was when he'd been drinking. How hurtful he was to Momma and me. Or how I felt about you. That was the biggest lie, seeing you every day and knowing you'd never feel the same way."

"You never asked." Now his words held a shade of regret, the same emotion she felt down to her toes.

"No, I didn't. It was easier that way. At least the me I was then thought so. I saw things in such stark black and white. No allowances for anything in the middle, so there wasn't a reason to question it."

"And now?"

"Now I know that talking is healthy. Asking questions is how certainty is defined. Conversations are critical to enhancing relationships. And secrets are a sure recipe for disaster."

"Yeah," he whispered, twisting his neck to look down at her. "Every word of that is true."

They stayed like that for a moment that extended into two, then five, then more. Mya slowed her breathing to match his, holding his gaze in the bravest thing she thought she'd ever done.

"Did you know Paul was gay?"

Mya shook her head. "Not until you guys went to the prom together."

"He asked me if I thought it was worth tearing up friendships to live a truth-filled life. I told him hell yeah, it was, and we decided the biggest statement he could make was the prom. Then you asked me, and I couldn't say yes. Not if I was going to help him figure out his own mess. I thought I'd have time to explain, but you pulled back. We spent less time together, mostly because I tried to be there for him throughout the fallout. He was a good friend, but you were my best friend, and I thought you'd just know what was going on. Now I know how stupid that was, and I should have talked about it." Kade sucked in a hard breath, then blew out a thin stream of air. "He was my first kiss, but I didn't love him. By then, I knew that both sexes tripped my trigger, so going to prom on Paul's arm was a way to be my own flavor of real. But I can guarantee you he wasn't the person I wanted to be there with that night. He wasn't the one I wanted to slow dance with." Kade tipped his head and brushed another kiss against her temple. "In case you're wondering, need more definitive proof? That person was you, Mya."

"You never said anything." She'd lost the fight against the slow trickle of tears minutes ago, and Kade's hand cupped her cheek, thumb brushing across the wet skin.

"Neither did you. Not one thing. But hell, Mya, we were both just kids. Kids who didn't have the best of anything, not with your dad's struggles and the death of mine. I think it would have been shocking if we hadn't sabotaged our own happiness at some point." His thumb glided along the curve of her eyebrow. "I believe it's a miracle we didn't shit-talk ourselves out of even friendship. Kids are dumb, sometimes. Real dumb."

"I think I was afraid."

"Not too afraid to strike out on your own. Hell, that's pretty damn fearless. And look at all you've accomplished in spite of everything. You're amazing, Mya. I'm so proud to call you my friend."

"I thought a clean break would be easier, but it wasn't. Those first couple years were hard."

"Hard at home too. You broke my heart." He said the words so calmly, she had to study his features to find the truth there. That had to be the pain she'd seen before, the flashes of anger. "I was so mad at you. I kept thinking that surely, you'd come back. That you couldn't be really gone. So I hung around. Certain you'd come to your senses from whatever wild hair you'd had. I mean, of course, I needed to make sure my baby brother made it through school, keep him on the straight and narrow. But behind everything was my hope you'd show back up someday. Man, was I ever gonna give you a piece of my mind. Had the speech all planned out, all the things I needed to tell you, all the anger I was gonna drown you in. I wrote it all down. Filled a dozen notebooks with rage." He snorted a soft laugh. "Then when I did see you, all that fell to the side, because all I could think about was there you were. Right there. In touching distance. And I promised myself it would be different this time. Angry me was a child, but the man holding you now? He's in love with you. After all this time, that emotion is still my core truth."

"I'd understand if you felt differently."

His hand cupped her chin, lifting and angling so his lips met hers in a soft caress. "And I'd understand if you did too. The good thing is we've both had those intervening years to grow up. Gain perspective." Kade gently nipped her bottom lip. "And here we are now."

Bo jumped on the couch cushion next to Mya's legs, and Kade made an impatient noise.

"What?" she asked, keeping her gaze fixed on his face.

"Dogs are h-u-n-g-r-y. Which means I need to move, and I just don't want to." His fingers glided along her jaw, slipping back to tangle his fingers in her hair. "I kinda like this."

"Me too." She snuggled closer to his chest, wrapping her arms around his neck in a loose hold. "But if they're hungry—"

Three barks and one baying howl split the air, and Mya jerked in surprise before falling into a giggling fit.

"Now you did it. You said the word that's almost as bad as t-r-e-a-t-s." Kade laughed as they were bounced around on the couch, dogs jumping over each other to gain attention.

"What? Treats?" The cacophony of sound grew in volume, until she couldn't hear Kade's laughter but still felt every movement as his chest heaved and shuddered underneath her touch. "Okay, I see your point."

She tipped her head back, smiling up at him, not surprised when he immediately captured her mouth. Lids fluttering closed, she went willingly into the darkness, focusing on the certainty of his touch and caresses, the controlled hunger in his kisses. For a moment, all she could hear was the pounding of her own heart, the rasp of his stubble against her cheeks and chin, and the gentle sounds of arousal flooding from his lips.

"Killin' me here, honey." Kade pulled back slightly, and Mya's lids opened slowly to see his gaze fixed on her face, pupils wide, eyes blown dark with excitement. "Let me take care of the dogs, and we'll resume this, yeah?"

"Yeah," she agreed, pushing up the couple of inches to touch her mouth to his again. "I'll be here."

"Better not go anywhere, woman." He shuffled around underneath her, sliding her to one side. "Be right back."

Standing, he called the dogs, and she watched as his little pack scampered after him and into the kitchen. Cabinet doors opening and dishes clanking let her know his progress, followed by his gentle commands to the dogs, calling them one at a time to their dish for a fondle and dinner.

He's a good man.

The knowledge was soul deep inside her. The responsible teenager had grown to be a rock-steady man. Someone to lean on, someone to work beside for shared goals.

Don't get ahead of yourself, Mya.

She thought about the expression on his face when he'd patiently listened to her version and then shared his truth with honesty.

I don't think I am exaggerating things. I think it's exactly as it seems, and I'm here for it.

Kade appeared in the archway, fingertips reaching overhead to grip the frame above his head. He was studying her, appearing lost in thought as he stretched. He'd removed the leather vest worn on the bike. The hem of his shirt rode up a couple of inches in front, and Mya's body heated, a flush rushing through her that she was sure blazed on her face.

"Do you trust me?" He dropped his arms and bent over, tugging his boots off and tossing them to the side. His socks followed, and she got with the program, leaning to take off her own boots. It took longer because they were lace-ups, and when she looked up again, he was halfway to where she sat. "Mya? Do you trust me?"

"With everything inside me." She finished with her boots and socks, stretching out her hand at the same time his rose from his side towards her. "Always, Kade."

Fingers wrapping around her hand, he gently pulled, encouraging her to rise from the couch. After a single soft kiss, he took a step backwards, their hands bridging the gap between them, and she went willingly. Kade led her down the hallway to where she knew his bedroom was. At the doorway, he paused, turning to look down at her.

He crowded close, caging her in. Low and earnest, he told her, "I've never had a woman or man in this bed. Never wanted one in my space. There are no ghosts here to compare yourself to." His other hand rose to curl around the back of her neck. "I want you. Want to see you on my pillows. Want to go to sleep with you here. And more, God, more than anything, I want to wake up with you."

Mya let her emotions show on her face, a blooming pleasure that he'd worry about her feelings and the shy desire that was twisting her tongue into tangles.

Kade's head dipped down, and Mya rose on her toes, meeting him halfway. She didn't want to be a passive observer in whatever this was between them. No, she wanted to be fully engaged with whatever he was going to propose.

His tongue stroked across the seam of her mouth, and she chased it with her own, opening demandingly, wanting to taste him.

"God, Mya," he groaned, before their lips fit together, the kiss deepening, surging towards combustion with a steady beat, wet and heady. "Better than I dreamed." His mouth traced along her jaw and down her throat, teeth and lips competing for her attention, goose bumps and shivers accompanying every movement. "Every inch of you, honey. Wanna have my hands on you."

Mya arched backwards in his arms, reaching down to the hem of her shirt. She lifted, losing sight of his face for a moment, then as the fabric cleared her head, his expression blazed through her. Hunger, desire, and so much love. She tossed her shirt to the side and slipped her hands underneath his shirt, pulling it up his body. Mya lost the security of his arms as he helped, twisting and pulling to take off the clothing that was in both their way. Then he crushed her to him tightly, bodies fusing from hips to chest.

Kade looked down at her breasts, threatening to escape the binding of her bra. "Jesus, honey."

Removing the undergarment was the work of moments, and then there was nothing between his skin and hers. The heat was enormous, and the contrast of her pale skin against his tattoos was stark, the difference gorgeous.

Kade bent, taking one breast in a palm, lifting the nipple to his mouth. His lips closed around it, and the deep suckling movement made her knees weak. Fingers molding the flesh, mouth working against her, the image was one she wanted to tuck away and keep forever.

"Love that," she murmured, threading her fingers through his hair. She cradled his head against her with both arms, holding him gently as he transferred his attention from one breast to the other, the sensation no less staggering. The soft bristle of his beard gave a fascinating counterpoint to the sharp scrape of his teeth around her nipple, and she moaned softly.

He moved then, standing up and lifting her, taking three giant steps to the bed, where he followed her down. Mya fumbled with the clasp of his belt, and he took over, stripping it out of the loops and tossing it to the side with a metallic clank. Then she was working on the fastening of his pants, and his hands were at her waist.

With a laugh, she pulled back, smiling up at him. "Might go faster if we did our own?"

"Jesus, why can't clothes just fly off like in the movies?" he grumbled, rolling to the side to work his pants and briefs down his thighs.

Mya planted her heels in the mattress, lifting her hips to slip her own pants down her legs. "I don't know, but that's something we should look into."

Toenails clipped up the hallway, and Kade rolled his eyes. "Oh, no you don't, Bocephus. No cockblocking tonight." He jumped out of bed and slammed the door closed, turning to face her. "Jesus, Mya. Look at you, baby." His rigid cock rose between his thighs, aimed directly at her. It pulsed up and down, and she could see the veins throbbing along the bottom of his shaft.

"Nah, I only have eyes for you," she countered, using her elbows to shove herself farther up the mattress until her head hit the pillows. With a courage she'd never before possessed, Mya let her legs fall to the side and trailed a hand up her torso. Her nipples had pebbled, skin cool without him next to her.

That didn't last long, though, because Kade leapt on the bed beside her, both laughing when the jostling bounces rocked them together.

One hand settled at her waist, Kade propped himself up on an elbow, looking down into her face. He stayed in that position for a long breath, gaze flicking across her features and down her body.

"What?" Mya reached up to stroke her fingers through his short beard, using the tip of one finger to trace the shape of his lips.

"Every dream." Kade blinked, and she saw a gleam of moisture in his eyes. "Never thought I'd ever get to experience this with you."

"Past is past." She smiled when he nipped at her finger. "Now is now, Kade." He pressed a soft kiss to her finger, then nestled his face into her palm. "I want you."

"Well, never let it be said I didn't give the lady what she wanted." He stretched his hand out to the nightstand, and she heard rustling before he huffed with annoyance. She snorted in amusement when he moved to hover over her, still focused on his efforts. "Fuckin' finally," he muttered, slipping back into place next to her. He dropped a condom on her belly, and she had to laugh. "Just keepin' you safe, honey," he said softly, his face lowering to hers for another deep, endless kiss.

Mya bent one knee, and Kade didn't miss the invitation, his hand delving between her thighs, fingers slipping along her already-soaked center. "Oh, yes," she whispered, pressing kisses to every inch of skin she could reach. His head was angled to gain renewed access to her breasts, and the dual sensations tightened every muscle in her core. "Please, Kade," she called. "I'm close already."

"Tell me what you want, Mya. What do you need?" His mouth moved across her chest and down, lips caressing the soft skin of her belly.

"You, Kade. I need you. Want you inside me, please. Don't want to come without you." Mya moved restlessly, hips pumping up against his touch, needing more. "Please."

"I got you." He shifted to his knees between her thighs, his hand still covering her core. Tearing the wrapper open with his teeth, he attempted to don the condom using just one hand, scowling when it was too hard.

"Let me." She took it from him, pinching a generous segment at the tip before placing it at the head of his cock. Rolling it down slowly, she teased the base of his erection with her fingertips, slipping down farther to roll his balls in her palm.

"Jesus." He gave a full body jerk, his cock dipping and twitching. "You can't do that, honey. I'm on a hair trigger as it is." Kade curled one hand behind her thigh, lifting her leg to place her ankle on his shoulder. "Wanna see, Mya. Let me see, baby."

Staring up at him, Mya nodded wordlessly, lids fluttering closed when she felt him notch the head of his cock against her opening.

"Look at me, honey. Wanna know you see me. Only me."

She blinked and settled her gaze on his face, watching as his eyes flicked down to where they were slowly being joined. Down and up, down and up, as his broad cock eased forward in pulses, filling her. The stretch was so welcome, Mya's eyes filled. Not with pain but with a sense of completion.

"You okay?" He stared down at her, expression worried.

"Never better," she promised him. Biting her bottom lip, she tensed around his cock, loving the wild expression that flashed across his face. "Are you okay?"

"Jesus fuckin' Christ on a goddamn stick in a bastard shittalkin' storm." His eyes rolled up when she clamped down again, hips stuttering slightly. "I'm tryin' to be considerate here. Make sure you're good."

"Oh, Kade. I'm so good, I can't even imagine being better." Mya lifted her hips slightly, fucking herself on his cock. "But if you don't move soon, I can't be held responsible for my own actions."

"Oh, it's on, baby." He grinned down at her, the devilish expression not hiding the other emotion hovering just behind. "Prepare yourself."

"Oh, I'm prepar—"

One hand on her thigh, holding her leg against his chest, Kade moved, hips creating a tempo and rhythm she found matched her desire exactly. His hips pistoned forward and back, the glide of his cock in and out creating friction that lifted her heart skyward. His other hand landed low on her belly, thumb tucked tight to her clit as he flicked it at an unpredictable pace.

She gasped, her hands flying to grip his wrist, pulling his touch tighter, harder. "Kade?"

"Yeah, baby. Go. Go and fly for me." His chin dropped, gaze fixed on her face as their bodies moved together. "Wanna see you fly."

He shifted slightly, knees spreading wider, and the change in angle pummeled her in all the right ways. Mya couldn't have held back her orgasm if she'd wanted, but there was nothing she wanted more than this. Kade in bed with her. Kade inside her. Kade's words of love echoing in her head.

"Kade!" Her cries echoed in the room, his name the only word she could say, the "Please" echoing through on repeat. Pleasure pulsed through her, rocketing higher with every thrust of his cock. Toes curling, she arched her back but kept her gaze on him. "Anything for you," she cried. "Everything. Kade."

Toppling over the crest of the wave, she rode it down the other side, body on fire as he wrung every ounce of pleasure out of her.

Kade's movements slowed gradually, stilling when she tugged his thumb away from her clit, the torturous touch now too much.

Mya was breathing heavily, sweat covering her skin. Kade was the same; his chest rose and fell with hard breaths, his tattoos shining in the light.

"So good." It had been so much more than good, and she wanted him to know, but her mouth wouldn't cooperate yet. "So good."

"You're breathtaking, Mya." He eased her leg off his shoulder, letting it fall to rest beside his hip as he moved to cover her. They were still joined, and she felt another ripple of pleasure dance across her nerve endings as his cock throbbed. "Absolutely." He moved again, pushing up on both elbows, framing her face with his hands. "Breathtaking."

Mya turned her head to press a kiss to his palm, then looked up to see him closer. Their lips met in a gentle kiss, and he nibbled softly, tongue stroking into her mouth to tease hers.

"Ready for more, honey?"

Mya nodded, wrapping her arms around his neck. She pulled him down into a deeper kiss, hunger stirring inside her again at the taste. At the knowledge that she could do this, finally.

"Move, honey," she urged, rocking her hips up against him. "Wanna feel you."

"You got it." He matched movement to his words, stroking inside her with a languid shift of his pelvis.

They went on like that for an unmeasured time, kisses merging from one to the next as their bodies rippled and rolled together. She felt the shift when it happened for him, the urgency returning. His body pulled hers along for the ride, the ridges of his cockhead rubbing against every delectable nerve ending inside her.

His mouth moved to her neck, shoulder, then back to her neck, mouth coming to rest near her ear. Mya clutched a handful of hair in one hand, the other slipping down his body to cradle his ass. She pulled and pushed at the muscled flesh, urging him to a faster stroke, desperately chasing the sensations.

"Mya. My Mya." His words were breathless, heat gusting across her skin as he murmured her name in a hundred different combinations that all spoke to the same emotion.

Love.

When the thought burst in her brain, it was quickly followed by fireworks behind her eyelids, the shattering of her body for the second time coming on her unexpectedly. She stiffened, then moved faster, wrapping her legs around his hips.

"Love you" slipped from her mouth, and the catch of his breathing told her he'd heard everything she said and also what she'd meant. "So much."

"My Mya."

He groaned, thrusting wildly, rhythmless for a moment. Each powerful movement unleashed another wave of sensation.

She was so close, it didn't matter, rapidly falling into a rolling continuation of her second orgasm.

Kade buried himself deep and paused in place, breath and hips hitching hard as if he tried to climb inside her. She felt the heat and pulsing throb of his cock as he filled the condom. They stayed like that for a breath, locked together in a passion she'd never expected.

His arms slipped beneath her back, crushing her against his chest. She huffed, and Kade rolled them to the side, somehow staying joined. Mya pulled in a deep breath, then giggled softly. His cock twitched at the movement, and she giggled again.

"Can I just stay like this forever?" Using his bicep as a pillow underneath her cheek, Mya stared at him, letting her gaze trace his face, wanting to set every memory in stone. "I kinda like this."

"Me too." Kade sighed, the sound deeply content. "I'll clean us up in a minute." A yawn broke through, his jaw cracking with the wide movement. He hummed softly. "Yup. Just give me a minute."

"If I wake up glued to you, I'm gonna be mad."

"Honey, if you think you aren't already glued to me, you're not paying attention." Eyes closed, Kade smiled serenely. "Never letting you go."

His breaths evened out, face relaxing as he dozed, but the circle of his arms never loosened. Kade held her as close and tightly in his sleep as he had while making love, and she understood what he'd meant.

"You're assuming I'd want you to let me go," she whispered. Curling her hand around his arm, she nestled beside him. "And in case you're still listening, I never want that. Disallowed, sir."

Chapter Five

Kade

Kade woke with the scent of Mya in his lungs, the taste of her on his lips, and when he opened his eyes, he breathed deeply, relaxing at the realization it hadn't been a dream.

She was lying right here beside him, head angled on his arm, and her hands piously folded against his chest. Her neck bore the marks of beard burn, the rosy color declaring his conquest of her. *Finally I can breathe.*

A glance at the window told him they hadn't been sleeping long, and when he reached down to finally deal with the condom, he was glad. The latex pulled uncomfortably at his pubes, cold jizz and spermicide making a goo that coated his cock.

Rubber removed and tied off, he slipped towards the edge of the bed and stood, then bent and scooped Mya into his arms bridal style.

She made an adorable "Eeep" that pulled a laugh from him, and her arms wrapped around his neck, nearly choking tight.

"Easy, baby," he crooned, mouth to the side of her head. "Gonna get us a shower."

"Don't drop me." Her mumbled command was spoiled by another "Eeep" as he shifted her higher in his arms. "Kade!"

She halfheartedly slapped the side of his shoulder. "You did that on purpose."

"Who me?" Elbowing the bathroom door open, he fumbled for a towel to drape across the cabinet before setting her down. "I'm just tryin' to take care of you."

By the time the shower ran warm, she'd forgiven him, her legs looping around his waist as they kissed without urgency.

This. He pulled back and stared into her eyes. *This is what I've been missing my whole life.*

There'd been so many misunderstandings in their past, things each had been blind to, mostly attached to their young age and lack of world experience.

We've got a couple decades on those kids. Maybe our time wasn't then.

"What are you thinking about that's so serious?" Mya leaned an elbow on his shoulder, her fingers caressing gently along the edge of his jaw, nails gently scratching along his skin. Something he'd never known he'd like but now couldn't imagine doing without. Also, he couldn't imagine allowing anyone else these casual caresses.

"Wondering about our time, you know? It's now, and I feel that deep down in my gut. I don't want to waste another moment, though." He kissed her softly, then wrapped his palms around her ass and lifted her from the counter, turning to walk into the shower. "But all that can wait. Right now it's time to get you and me unsticky."

Washing her body was a revelation, a lesson in adoration. The acres of creamy skin with rivulets of water tracing each dip and curve were mesmerizing. She seemed to find the same fascination with water running down his chest and stomach. Her fingertips tracked along the many lines of his tattoos, following the sweep of color across his shoulders and back. The questions came rapidly, often overwriting the one preceding it until he couldn't answer any of them.

"What does this one stand for?"

"Did it hurt?"

"When did you get this one done?"

He finally captured her hands in his, twisting her in his arms so her back settled against his front. "Woman, if you don't stop touching me all over, we're gonna have shower sex. And I don't have condoms in here, so that's a no-go."

Mya laughed softly, chin tilting up to look at him over her shoulder. "We'd only need one for penetrative sex." She wiggled a hand free of his grip and slipped it behind her, cupping his cock and angling it between her thighs near the juncture of her core. He pushed as she rocked backwards, the flow of water easing his way. "See, we can do plenty of stuff without you putting on a raincoat."

"A raincoat, huh?" Nudging her cheek with his nose, he urged her to meet his mouth. Kissing her was like coming home; the intimate action made more precious because it was Mya. "You're right." He bent his knees slightly, changing the angle to skim across her sex lightly. "Don't need a condom for this." Kade glided a hand down her belly, fitting a finger to either side of her clit before pinching gently. Her moan was low and breathy, ending on a rising keen.

"Kade." She flung an arm up, curling her hand around the back of his neck, pulling herself closer for another deep, rousing kiss.

He felt the tremors rocketing through her and increased the pace of his movements, both hips and fingers. Keeping pace with her arousal was a dance he'd willingly spend the rest of his life learning. Their kisses changed into open-mouthed gasps. Her gaze locked with his in a way that felt like she saw all of him. All the good. All the bad. Everything that made him, she saw. Kade was raw but settled at the same time, vulnerable and dominating in the same breath.

"Coming," he told her, the uncoiling spring in his belly pushing him breakneck to the finish line. He coated the insides of her thighs, feeling the heat of his cum against his hand as he teased and tweaked her clit.

"Oh my God." Mya turned in his arms, every movement languid and graceful. "My knees are mush."

"I've got you." He wrapped an arm around her waist, using the cupped palm of the other to wash them off. "I've got you."

***

Mya

After the shower excursion, Kade had been determined to feed her. Once he'd decisively dressed her in one of his shirts, that was. With the hem of the T-shirt skimming along her thighs, Mya had enjoyed working alongside him in the kitchen. Throwing a couple of steaks on the grill and popping a pan of fries in the oven wasn't cooking, not really, but it had been nice to share even such mundane tasks with someone.

Not just someone. With Kade.

She agreed with her thoughts, wild though they felt sometimes. Kade had always made everything better, all across the board. That wasn't anything new, but the feeling of strength she now had with him standing beside her was. Not fragile or tentative, but solid. Firm. Something she knew she could depend on.

After food, they'd settled on the couch and watched a couple of episodes of some reality show neither was really interested in. Touches and caresses filled the moments with far more enjoyment than whatever manufactured drama was playing out on the screen. Even the fact the dogs were all lounging around made it better. It was a homey slice of time, and Mya wanted a thousand more moments like those.

Going to bed had been another revelation, because while they didn't have sex again, Kade's arms around her were as intimate as it got. His hands had skimmed along her sides, up and down her arms, finally pausing to twine their fingers together.

Now she'd woken with his breath ghosting across the nape of her neck, in an echo of the first time she'd woken with him. Her first love finally in her bed.

Well, I'm in his bed now. But I think it still counts.

"You awake?" The rumble of his question came from beside her ear, and Mya turned her head to look at him.

"I am. How'd you sleep?" Her eyes dipped shut as his mouth dropped to hers, cutting off any additional conversation. Even closed-mouthed, the connection between them buzzed and vibrated, the soft sighs he hummed against her lips an adorable addition.

"Like a baby. Somethin' about you makes it all good." He pushed up on an elbow and tugged at her waist, turning her to face him. "How'd *you* sleep? Strange bed and all. Did you sleep okay?"

"Very well. Best in a while." *Since I last woke in your arms,* she thought but didn't voice. "I woke just a minute ago." Tracing down the ridge of his nose with a fingertip, she let her touch linger on his lips, smiling when he pressed a kiss to them. "Do you have coffee?"

"Not on me, no." Tongue trapped between his teeth, he grinned at her. "But in the kitchen, yes. I'll make a pot in a minute."

"Make a pot? You don't have one of the pod machines? How very caveman of you."

"I drink too much coffee to make one of those worth it." He bent and nuzzled along the side of her neck, lips working her skin. "I gotta say, I like wakin' up like this, Mya."

"Me too." Caught up in a wave of emotion, she blurted, "I'd do nearly anything to have this with you all the time."

"Well, good for you, I'm not charging any kind of admittance. See—" His mouth trailed along her collarbone, teeth gently nipping. "I'm kinda in the same place, honey. Want you here, or wanna be in your place."

"Dogs are here," she muttered, arching her neck, hoping to get more caresses.

"That they are." His lips moved against her throat, and she just knew he was smiling. "Are you sayin' you'd come here just to be with my dogs?"

"Well, you're a package deal, right?" Twisting her fingers in his hair, she pulled until he lifted his head and looked at her. She'd been right: he was grinning widely. "Don't look so smug. Bo's a good boy."

"Just love me for my dogs," he whispered, tone regretful. "Hurts me right in the feels."

"No, Kade. I love you for you. Bo's a plus."

"Say it again." His voice dropped an octave, gaze fixed on her face, his eyes intense. "Say it again, Mya."

"I love you."

Kade wrapped his arms around her and fell to his side, pulling Mya with him as he rolled until she was sprawled out on his chest. "Will never, ever get tired of you sayin' that, baby. Not ever." He cradled her head, fingers threading into her hair on each side as he pinned her in place. His chest was heaving hard, each indrawn breath lifting her as they stared at each other. "Love you so fuckin' much, Mya. Fuckin' love you."

"And you forgive me?" When his brows scrunched together, she elaborated, "For making us waste so much time?"

"Oh, honey." He pulled her down for another kiss, this one deeper, renewing until he broke it off and glided his mouth to her ear. "Like I said, I think this is meant to be our time. Neither of us were ready before. Now, though? We're in it to win it, baby."

"I'm so glad you didn't give up on me." When he scowled and opened his mouth, she cut him off with a finger across his lips. "And that's all I'll say on the topic. I get what you're saying, and just knowing how I've grown and changed since we were in school, I think you're right. But I can still be grateful for life bringing us back together when we were both in the right space to be here."

"Even if it took a wreck to get us back on track?" He nipped at her finger, grinning when she pulled in a startled breath. Mya pressed her pelvis downwards, feeling his cock slowly uncoiling at her hip. "Don't answer that." He rolled them again, legs slotting deftly between her thighs. "I've got other ideas for the next little bit."

"I like your ideas." Mya arched up against him, relishing how the firm planes of his chest molded her breasts. "You're a genius, my friend."

"Lemme show you just how much of a genius I can be."

For the next hour, he did just that, until she was sated, sweaty, and shaking, slowly recovering in his arms.

***

Kade

"I know you."

Kade turned at the confidently spoken statement and found himself facing someone he definitely didn't know. He studied the man, and made the connection.

"Doctor Taylor, I presume?" The man matched Mya's scant description of "you can't miss him" making sense.

His grin in response made Kade like him already.

"Yes, sir." The grin fell away, leaving him scowling in its place. "And you better not ever forget me. I'm the best friend, and I know things about you that should never reach the light of day."

"What?" Kade was taken aback by the direct attack.

"I'm a doctor. I can do things people don't expect." The smaller man stepped forwards, edging into Kade's space. "I can have you involuntarily committed in less than an hour, held for 72 hours, and get a judge to sign a paper giving me authority over you." He tipped his chin up. "I'm the gay best friend and you better get used to it."

"Man, you need to take a step back before these people get more of a show than they expected." Kade was the one inching forward this time. "I'm the boyfriend and partner, and you better fuckin' get used to it. Mya is mine, and while I'll understand your position as her friend, you better understand I will fuck you up if you do anything to sabotage what I'm building with her." He was shocked when his statement was met with a broad smile.

Lawrence Taylor backed away a step and thrust out his hand. "I'm Law, and I'm so incredibly glad to meet you. Mya means the world to me, and I'm glad to know she's getting everything she ever wanted." He arched an eyebrow as he said, "She's not telling me much personal stuff, but from looking at you," his gaze trailed down and back up, "I'll happily make up the activities she's redacting."

"Whiplash." Kade grabbed his hand and pumped once, then pulled the man in for a one-armed hug. "That's your new name around me. Whiplash."

Law pulled away, looking startled. "Excuse me?"

"You gave me whiplash, so you're Whiplash. What is difficult to understand. You sure you're the other Doctor Taylor?"

"Oh, I see. Is this so your biker buddies will accept me as one of their own?"

"Nope. It's so I can watch the tips of your ears burn bright with embarrassment as you have to explain to everyone what the name means."

"What's your biker name, big guy?"

"K-man," he flicked a mocking salute. "At your service, sir. No weird names for me." He leaned in and waggled his eyebrows. "Just you."

"What's Mya's biker name?"

"Mya."

"But that's her normal name. What do your biker buddies call her."

"Mya."

"Why do I have to have a biker name and Mya doesn't?"

Kade felt a hand slip around his side and he automatically lifted his arm, wrapping it around Mya's shoulders.

"Mya doesn't have to have a biker name to belong. Mya just belongs." She was smiling as she made the statement. "Why do you have a biker name, and what is it?"

"Nothing." Law leaned close and gave her an air kiss. "Nothing at all."

"Say what you want, Whiplash, but the name's gonna stick."

Chapter Six

Kade

Pulling into the clubhouse's parking lot, Kade scanned the cars and trucks in the visitor's lot, smiling when he saw Mya's parked close to the front. He angled around the building to where members parked their bikes and backed into the space reserved for him.

Before he was even off the bike, he caught the crunching of gravel and looked to the side in time to see Mya running around the corner and straight towards him. Barely getting the helmet off before she landed in his arms, he dangled it from the handlebars as he lifted her, placing her crosswise on the tank in front of him. Mya's arms went around his neck, and she tugged him in for a kiss, her mouth demanding as it met his.

"Hey, baby," he whispered when they finally broke apart, breathing ragged. "I'm thinkin' you missed me?"

"I'm never ever going to another weeklong conference. I don't care how many continuing education units it gets me. I'll study something at home on the couch next year instead." She folded against his chest, head resting on his shoulder as she sighed deeply. "I missed you, yes. In case that wasn't clear."

"I kinda got the message." Kade tightened his hold around her, loving the feel of Mya in his arms. "I missed you too."

"What do you think about me giving up my lease entirely?"

The question seemed to come from left field, but Kade knew it was a decision Mya had struggled with. She'd liked the closeness of her bungalow to the clinic where she worked, but over the past three months, she'd spent few nights there.

And most of those, I'd been right in bed beside her anyway.

Since they'd reconnected in a big way, both Kade and Mya had jealously guarded their time together. Not wanting to make up for lost time, but just unwilling to let any distance come between them.

"I think payin' the lease is mad, especially when we both know what we want long term."

"Yeah," she whispered, settling more solidly against his chest. "I know what I want."

"Me too. And this is it. This being us, you know?"

"Plus, I don't think the neighbors would appreciate the Hazzard gang too much, especially Rosco." Mya giggled, the sound light and happy. "He's a noisy feller when he's riled up."

"That he is." Kade slid a hand up her spine to cradle the back of her head, fingers tangling in her hair as he tilted her face up. Their lips met in a soft, slow kiss, the caress centering him as it always did. "Takes after his daddy that way. I get loud when I'm riled up too."

"Oh, are you?" She grinned against his lips, and he kissed her through the smile. "I'd never have known."

"Woman." His fake stern tone earned another giggle, and he slapped her ass gently. "Slide off. Let's head inside and have a beer with the brothers." She wiggled out of his lap and stood beside the bike as he set the kickstand. "Ready?"

"Yes, sir." She saluted him with two fingers, then slipped her hand into his, their palms connecting as he wrapped his fingers around hers. "Ready and willing."

"I'll remember that for later. Did you ask the other Dr. Taylor if he wanted to stop by?"

Kade had liked the man the moment they'd met, and knowing how much he'd supported Mya through the years had solidified their quick friendship.

"I did. He said he'd rather meet everyone out at our place, which means we need to plan a cookout."

He tugged her to a stop and pulled her into his arms, bending his neck to crush his mouth to hers. Mya opened readily, and their tongues danced and glided, the kiss deep and wet. Kade didn't break the kiss until she was trembling and gasping for breath, and he placed his mouth next to her ear to whisper, "Fucking mine. My Mya. Our place. Our home. You sayin' that makes me happy, honey. Let's move you soon as we can."

"Okay," she agreed on a giggle, sounding kiss drunk. "You like hearing it and I like saying our place. Ours. We're building the best kind of thing here, Kade."

Hand to his chest, she reared back to stare up into his face.

The love for him was clear in her expression, a look so soft and real it brought him close to tears.

Arms tight around her, he swayed them side to side as he hummed. Her hand rose to curl around his shoulder, and she kept pace with his movements.

They danced that way, slow and sweet, until Torch opened the back door of the clubhouse to shout at them to come inside already.

"All the slow dances, Mya." He made the promise as he dipped for another kiss. "For the rest of our lives."

"I'm here for it." She took a deep breath, the air hitching a half dozen times as she pulled it in. "Slow dances, bike rides, dog walks, reality TV, cookouts—everything. I'm here for it."

"Will you come in already, Prez?" Torch called from the open doorway.

"You're interrupting something important, asshole," Kade responded without looking away from Mya's face, watching as her eyes crinkled at the corners.

"Jesus. Nobody gives me any respect anymore. Fucking stay outside until the cows come home. Suit yourselves." The door slammed closed, and Kade grinned.

"Now, where were we?"

"Confessions of everlasting love." Mya's hand moved so her fingers could twist in his hair. "I think that's where the placemark is."

"Put a pin in it, because if you're here for it, so am I. Doubled. Tripled. I'm here for all of it."

"I love you, Kade Martinez."

"And I'm fuckin' grateful, because I love you too."

Chapter Seven

Kade

All around them, the clubhouse buzzed with the low hum of voices and the clink of beer bottles as Kade leaned against the bar, Mya tucked close under his arm. Only a few months since the crash, and she'd slotted into his life not just like she'd never left, but like he'd never known he needed. Every day, her laughter was a balm to the rough edges of his days.

The Eusebeia's Pets MC had welcomed her too, Torch verbally sparring with her like she'd been born to it. Even better, the old ladies had taken to swapping stories over plates of grilled meat with her, as if she'd always been here.

She just fit. In the club, in his close friend circle, in his whole life. *Fuck yeah. I'm here for it.*

Tonight was a rare calm, a Friday where the only plan was drinking and bullshit.

"Another?" Mya nudged his bottle, her grin teasing.

"Only if you're pourin', honey." He kissed her temple, savoring the trusting way she leaned into him.

The back door banged open, cutting through the noise and drawing Kade's attention. Torch strode in, the expression on his face tight, his boots leaving grit on the floor. "K-Man, brother, we need you outside. Now."

Kade's gut clenched. His VP didn't spook easy, but this was the man with his hackles up. "Stay here," he murmured to Mya, sliding off the stool. She nodded, but her eyes stared up at him, her gaze sharp with worry.

Outside, the night air slipped past, cool against his skin. Torch led him to the prospects' bike lot, where half a dozen brothers stood in a loose circle, faces grim. Jimmy, one of the newest and barely patched Pets prospects, stood in the center. He shifted nervously, blood slowly trickling from a split lip. The bruises and injuries Kade could see had been inflicted within the past hour, putting a timer on whatever had gone down.

"What's this?" Kade demanded, stopping on the edge of the circle, his voice low.

"Waterfront Reapers," Torch spat. "They caught this dumbass ridin' too close to their turf. WRMC roughed him up, then sent him back with a message."

Kade stared at Jimmy. "What's the message. Word for fucking word, hear me?"

Jimmy swallowed hard. "He, Vance, their President, said 'The Pets fucking so-called charity runs are cuttin' into my business. Y'all are gonna stop roaming around. You work a product run in my territory, and you fucking know where I rule, so it means you're asking for my attention. Fucking stay east of the river or this is gonna become personal'."

Kade's jaw tightened. The Reapers were a festering sore. They were a bunch of drug runners and petty tyrants who'd been itching for a fight since the Pets started cleaning up the club image with their fundraisers. The Pet's weren't squeaky clean, they did a variety of for-profit runs. But the only time they'd come close to the WRMC territory had been the charity things. He stared at Jimmy, noting how the man's posture hadn't changed since he'd walked up. That likely meant only one thing. "They tag you?"

Shifting tentatively, eyes cast to the ground, Jimmy reluctantly lifted his shirt, revealing a crude WR carved into his side with a blade. Like his lip, blood still trickled down, slowly. Kade cursed under his breath, joined by every man.

"Goddammit. And goddamn them straight to hell. You're gonna need a couple of stitches, brother. We'll get you taken care of." Kade's stomach churned thinking of the process leading up to Jimmy enduring the slow slicing of his skin. *Can fucking bet it was slow as molasses. Bastards would love to stretch out the pain.*

"We can't let this slide," Torch said, eyes blazing. His hand came down on Jimmy's shoulder, holding steady. "This is goddamned bullshit. We let this go, next it'll be worse. They're testin' us."

"Agreed," Kade growled. "But we don't rush in blind. We'll call an all-patches church for tomorrow. Gotta bring in all the brothers. Jimmy, prospect or not, we'll need you there. You're the voice of this, man. We gather, we plan, and then we fucking kick the WRMC in the balls. But it starts with planning this right."

Back inside, Mya's gaze locked on him the second he crossed the threshold. She didn't speak, didn't ask, just slipped her hand into his, grounding him as the tension in his gut coiled tighter.

"Need me to get you a fresh beer?" Mya asked softly, leaning against his shoulder.

"No, babe." The last thing he needed tomorrow was a hangover. "Know what? Just a soda would be good."

"You got it." She pushed off and made her way to the bar, tonight tended by hangarounds.

Kade watched the man who approached her, noting how the man gave her an up-and-down look, then blanched slightly.

Torch laughed. "Asshole just tagged whose old lady she was. I'd say your reputation precedes you, and is growing." All humor left his voice as he continued, "That's fucking bullshit, what the WRMC did to Jimmy. Tagging him like that. They knew they'd be poking the bear. They're gonna be ready for us to throw something at them."

"Yeah," Kade agreed. "But remember, they're a club led by idiots who recruited more idiots to fill the ranks. The only thing they have on us is numbers. But like I said, they're idiots." He gripped Torch's hand, pulling him into a warrior's clench. "Good for us, we don't have a single idiot on the roster. They're gonna be ready for something, but we could give them a dozen days of warning and they still wouldn't be ready for us."

"Goddamn right. Pets are gonna fuck them up." Torch pulled back and Kade locked in on Mya, dancing her way back across the clubhouse main room, hands full with two glasses. "She's a keeper. Know I've said that before, but I'm goddamned glad you found your old lady."

"Me, too, brother. Best night of my life was realizing who I was there to rescue. She's mine." Kade leaned one elbow on the edge of the table. "And I'm a lucky man."

"What?" Mya leaned in and placed two drinks on the table. "Soda for you, and I got Torch a new whisky soda."

Torch slugged Kade's shoulder, barely pulling the hit. "Lucky fucking man."

***

Mya

Mya woke with a start, reaching out to an empty bed, Kade's side cool. The faint rumble of pipes outside told her he'd just left the house. She glanced at her phone. He'd ridden out early.

She padded to the kitchen, Bo nudging her leg as she brewed a fresh pot of coffee. The past week everything had seemed strained. Not between the two of them, but in the air around them. Kade had been noticeably quieter, and those easy smiles she lived for were far rarer since that night at the clubhouse. He'd told her a little about the WRMC, but she wasn't stupid. She knew he'd tamed down that description, trying to keep her from worrying. It hadn't worked. Tension hung over the house like a storm cloud.

Her phone buzzed. She saw it was Karen, and when she answered the woman started talking before Mya even got out a hello. "You alive out there in biker land?"

"Barely," Mya teased, though her chest tightened. "Kade's been … busy. I'm ready for things to settle down again."

"Busy with biker stuff?" Karen's tone sharpened. "Hey, I heard some whispers downtown. There's a rough crew been stirring shit up."

Mya frowned, her stomach churning. "What'd you hear?"

"Just bar talk. But it sounded serious. It was something about a rival gang flexing muscle all around town. Be careful, okay?"

"It's a club."

"What?" Karen sounded distracted.

"You called it a gang. It's a club. The differentiation matters."

"Whoa, Nelly." She had Karen's full attention again. "It wasn't an intentional cut. Just echoing things I've heard others say."

Mya giggled. "A cut is the vest they wear once they're patched into the club." She laughed softly. "Sorry, I've been trying hard to stay with the language I hear, so I get it."

***

When Kade rolled in hours later, dust streaked his jeans, and his expression was raw. He kissed her hard, like he needed to prove she was real. "Rough day?" she asked, keeping it light.

"Club business," he muttered, avoiding her eyes. "Nothin' for you to worry about."

She gripped his hand, stopping him. "I'm not fragile, Kade. Talk to me."

He sighed, sinking onto the couch. "Reapers hit one of our supply runs. Busted up a prospect, took the cash. We're ridin' out tomorrow to push back."

Her pulse spiked. "Push back how?"

"Show of force. No blood if we can help it. But if we're pushed, there's gonna be pain. Not for you, or any of the other old ladies. Not you." His thumb brushed her cheek. "I'll keep you safe, Mya. Promise."

She nodded, swallowing the fear. This was his world. And now hers. She needed to find her point of contribution. Like with the practice, she had to carve out somewhere that fit just her.

***

Kade

The river glinted under the noon sun as twenty Pets bikes roared west, Kade at the front beside Torch. Mya's face had been pale but her expression steady as he kissed her goodbye, and it haunted him. He'd left her with Bo and a burner phone, orders to call the clubhouse if anything felt off.

The Reapers' turf loomed ahead, a stretch of rundown bars and warehouses they'd claimed as their kingdom. It was a part of the city no one would normally contest their right to control, but starting today Kade was willing to throw down in order to run the Reapers out of town.

He raised a fist and the column stopped about a mile out, leaving engines idling. Torch walked his bike up next to Kade and they both scanned the horizon. "They'll know we're here. Gotta know we were gonna answer their bullshit."

"Good," Kade said. "Let 'em sweat. I want them to come to us."

Less than thirty minutes later, the Reapers rolled up—fifteen strong, led by a wiry bastard named Vance. *We've got better than one-on-one coverage.* Kade noted the president's cut was stained with grease and blood. *Sloppy, that's a lotta DNA on that vest.* "You're on our dirt, Martinez," Vance sneered.

"Your boys cut into ours first," Kade shot back. "Carvin' up a kid? A kid wearing my fucking patch? That's your play?"

Vance shrugged. "Message delivered. Back off the charity shit. It's bad for business."

Kade's fists clenched. "Your business is bullshit. We don't bow to trash. Push us again, and you'll feel it. Hell, you might not even have to push. Just a tap would be enough to unleash hell."

Vance's grin was all teeth. "Big words. Hope your lady likes hospital food. Mya, right? Real looker."

The direct threat hit deep, slicing through his control. Kade lunged, but Torch hauled him back. "Not here," he hissed. The Reapers peeled out, laughter echoing. Kade's blood boiled—Mya's name in that scum's mouth was a line crossed.

***

Mya

The burner phone rang, startling Mya so she nearly threw it.

"Hello?"

To her relief it was Kade's voice on the call. "Mya, the president of the Reapers laid out a threat to you. I want to take it seriously. Lock all the doors, make sure the dogs are inside with you."

"Threat to me?" She was already moving to the nearest outside entrance, engaging the locks. "Why would they even know about me?"

"Baby, I'm the President of the Pets, of course he knows. Are the dogs inside?"

Mya dropped her empty hand and felt various noses touching her fingertips. "Yeah, all four of the Hazzard famous are present."

"Okay, you stay like that, locked tight. Stay put, baby. I'll be there soon as I can."

The call disconnected and she stared at the phone.

How is this even real?

Mya paced Kade's living room, the burner phone heavy in her pocket. The dogs sensed her nerves, Luke whining at her feet. She'd tried to settle into her work, loading up software to make notes on a patient's file. Her mind kept spinning off back to Vance's threat, the little bit of knowledge Kade had laid out replaying in her head over and over. He'd told her to lock the doors, and stay put. She was doing that, but damn, she hated the waiting.

The dogs started growling and Mya's head snapped up when she heard a crunch of gravel under tires. Through the window, she saw a black van idling at the start of the dark tree line. She strained her eyes but could not make out a license plate, or any other markings. Nothing at all to tell her who might be inside. Her heart slammed against her ribs. Mya grabbed the phone, texting Kade:

*Van outside. Don't know who.

The message simply said "Delivered" but she received no reply. She watched as the van's side door slid open, and two figures stepped out. One was short, one tall, both wearing leather vests. The tall one turned and she saw the Waterfront Reapers patch glint in the glow cast by the security light. Mya's breath caught. She bolted to the kitchen, and snagged a knife from Kade's block, dropping her other hand to be back of Bo's neck. The dog was beside her, growling steadily. The front door rattled, and Mya heard wood splinter under a second heavy bang, quickly followed by another fierce blow against the door.

"Come on out here, bitch!" one shouted. *That cinches it, the threat Kade was afraid of was real.*

Mya crouched behind the counter, dialing Kade, nearly screaming when she got only voicemail again. Still outside, she heard multiple men laughing, then glass shattering somewhere along the West side of the house. *They're in the dining room.* Her heart began to pound. Bo lunged, Mya missing her snatch at his collar, and the dog was snarling as he swept out of the room. He disappeared, which was followed closely by a sharp yelp. The snarls escalated, paired with loud barks. Luke followed, while Daisy stayed with Mya. There was another pained yelp and Mya imagined a boot meeting fur, them kicking one of her dogs...her family. An immediate and overwhelming rage overtook the fear. She pushed to her feet, knife raised, and screamed, "Get out!"

The taller one smirked, Bo staying just out of kicking range. The man began advancing, pushing Bo back towards Mya— until the roar of bikes split the air. If a noise could convey emotion, this would be wrath. The two Reapers in the house froze, then bolted as Kade's club tore into the clearing surrounding his house, their home. The three King Shepards chased the men all the way to the vehicle, and Mya watched as the van somehow split the group of bikes and escaped up the drive. *Doesn't matter. Long as they're gone.* She sank to the floor as Kade burst in, wild-eyed.

"You okay?" He dropped beside her, hands everywhere, checking. "Baby, talk to me."

"Yeah," she gasped, clinging to him. "I'm fine, honey. They didn't touch me." Bo skidded around the end of the counter, crowding in beside Kade so he could lick the tears off her face. "I'm find. As long as you're okay, I'm fine."

His jaw clenched, muscles working as he ground teeth together. "They are gonna fucking pay for this."

"They didn't hurt me. They didn't touch me, didn't get the chance. The dogs made sure of that. Check Bo, I think one of them kicked him. He was defending me."

One of Kade's hands roamed over Bo, conducting an inspection by feel. "He's a good boy. Did his job."

"The best boy," she agreed.

The other three dogs crowded around, and Mya gave each love as she could reach them, but Kade wouldn't relinquish his hold on her.

Torch came into view and studied them for a minute. "You good, Mya lady?"

She nodded and Kade gave her a squeeze.

"We get a name or plate on those assholes?" Kade's voice sounded rough, like he'd been screaming for hours. "We know who they are?"

"We did, and we do, Prez. Their patches were real, and cameras showed them sliding into the WRMC compound about two minutes ago." Torch squatted down, one knee on the floor, arms crossed on his other leg. "We rolling or we strategizing?"

"Strategizing," Kade answered immediately and Mya felt a little of the tension leave her.

"I'm glad." Her whisper had both men looking at her. "The club acts as a unit, or it's just a bunch of individual people who like bikes. The unit scenario is much harder, but it's beneficial in the long run. When everyone feels like they have a say, then they have skin in the game." She shook her head. "Sorry, stress apparently sets me straight into presentation mode." She snuggled against Kade's shoulder a little closer. "I'm good, and I'll be good, because I understand that I'm not alone. Doesn't matter if I ride in front or in back, the club will be on my side. On Kade's side. Because that's just what family does."

"You're fuckin' smart, did you know that?" Kade gave her a squeeze. "Let's all head back to the clubhouse. Torch we need one of the prospects to drive my truck. We'll get the dogs loaded up before we pull out. The way he's watching her right now, I suspect Bo'll follow the bike if he got the chance." He straightened slightly and looked down at Mya. "You're on the back of my bike, baby. Need to know you're okay."

"No arguments from me. I need you close too."

Chapter **Eight**

Kade

Club church was active and loud that night, the strained atmosphere thick with cigarette smoke and fury. Mya sat upstairs with the old ladies. It killed Kade not to have her nearby, but he knew she was safe even if very shaken still.

Kade slammed a fist on the table, taking out a little bit, just the tiniest amount of his rage. "They came to my house. Threatened my woman. This has to end now."

Torch nodded. "My vote is we target their warehouse. Burn their stash. They'll feel it in their pockets."

"Risky," said Dirteater, the club's Enforcer, his name a misnomer. "Cops'll sniff around."

"Worth it," Kade snarled. "WRMC crossed a line. A big goddamned fucking line. Old ladies and families are not to be touched. They were seconds away from putting their goddamned hands on mine."

Torch lifted a hand, "All in favor, we ride out tonight. All not in favor, take your pansy ass back home and expect to have your patch rescinded. As in removed from your backs. Anyone taking that route?" Silence swirled through the room, much like the smoke expelled in the air.

"Okay then." Kade stood, palms flat on the tabletop. "Get going, brothers. Kiss your babies and hug your old ladies. I'd like for everyone vulnerable to be under this roof before we roll out. We'll pick a good contingent to protect our most precious."

At midnight, ten Pets rode out, Kade's blood singing with vengeance. The Reapers' warehouse loomed into view, the weary building a rotting shell by the docks. The Pets moved fast. Molotov's flew through windows, flames licking up the inside walls. Kade watched it catch fire, staying a moment to watch it burn, Mya's trembling hands in his mind.

Back at the clubhouse, he found her outside on the porch, sitting with Bo at her side. She didn't speak, just fondled Bo's ears with a gentle touch.

"It's done," he said, voice rougher than he meant, stepping closer. "They won't touch you again."

Mya's eyes lifted, locking onto his. They weren't soft, not tonight. They were molten, sharp with something that wasn't fear or relief but a challenge, a spark that dared him to close the distance. "I'm not running, Kade," she said, her voice low, steady, like she was staking a claim. "We're not going to run, ever. This is us now."

He stopped an arm's length away, his hands flexing at his sides. The urge to haul her up, to press her against the wall and feel every inch of her under his hands, was a living thing clawing at his chest. But he held back, letting the tension coil tighter, the air between them thick with everything unsaid. Her lips parted, just a fraction, and he caught the quick rise of her chest, the way her fingers tightened in Bo's fur like she was grounding herself too.

"Us," he echoed, the word a vow. He stepped closer, slow, deliberate, until the toes of his boots brushed her bare feet. She didn't move, didn't flinch, just tilted her head up, her gaze never leaving his. The porch light carved shadows across her face, and fuck, she was beautiful, wild and unbroken, even after tonight. Especially after tonight.

"You were scared," he murmured, not a question, his voice dropping to a growl that vibrated in his throat. He crouched down, eye-level now, his hands braced on the arms of her chair, caging her without touching. Not yet. "I saw it in your eyes when I got there. But you stood your ground, knife in hand, ready to take them down."

Her lips twitched, a ghost of a smile, but her eyes burned. "Had to," she said, her voice catching just enough to make his blood heat. "Couldn't let them think I'd break. Not when I'm yours."

That word hit him like a fist, her gently spoken *"yours"* unraveling the last thread of his control. He leaned in, close enough to feel the warmth of her breath, the faint scent of her skin, a sweet vanilla paired with something sharper, like the edge of a storm. "Damn right you're mine," he said, his voice a low rasp, every syllable heavy with need. "And I'm yours, Mya. Every fucked-up piece of me."

Her hand lifted, hesitating for a heartbeat before her fingers grazed his jaw, the touch light but electric, sending a jolt straight through him. Her thumb brushed the corner of his mouth, and he turned his head just enough to catch it, his lips pressing against her skin. Her breath hitched, a small sound that made his pulse roar. He wanted to hear it again, wanted to pull every sound from her. Wanted to map every inch of her with his hands, his mouth, touch and caress her until the fear and the fire of tonight were burned away.

"Kade," she whispered, her voice a thread of want, and it was all he could do not to crush her to him right there. Her fingers slid into his hair, tugging just enough to make his scalp sting, and he groaned low, the sound vibrating between them. She leaned forward, her forehead brushing his, her breath warm against his lips, and the world narrowed to the heat of her, the way her body shifted closer, like she couldn't help it either.

"You keep lookin' at me like that," he said, his voice rough as gravel, "and I'm gonna forget we're on a porch with half my club inside."

"Let 'em hear," she shot back, her voice low, daring, and the challenge in it made his blood sing. Her fingers tightened in his hair, pulling him closer, and he let her, his hands finally finding her waist, gripping just hard enough to feel her warmth through her thin shirt. Her hips shifted, pressing into his hold, and he swallowed a curse, his thumbs brushing the bare skin just above her jeans.

"Careful, baby," he growled, his lips so close to hers he could almost taste her. "You're playin' with fire."

"Good," she said, her voice a husky challenge, her eyes locked on his. "Burn me."

He kissed her then, hard and hungry, like he could pour every ounce of his fear, his rage, his need into her. Her mouth opened under his, soft and fierce, her hands pulling him closer, nails biting into his neck. The kiss was a war, a promise, a claiming—her taste flooding his senses, her body arching into him like she was staking her own claim. He slid one hand up her back, fingers tangling in her hair, tilting her head to deepen the kiss, and she moaned, a soft, desperate sound that frayed his control.

Bo whined, nudging Kade's leg, and they broke apart, breathing hard, her lips swollen, her eyes dark with want. She laughed, a shaky sound, and pressed her forehead to his again. "Your dog's got shit timing," she muttered.

Kade chuckled, the sound rough, his hands still on her, not ready to let go. "He's just jealous," he said, brushing his lips against her jaw, feeling her shiver. "Thinks he's the only one who gets to protect you."

She tilted her head, giving him better access, her voice a whisper. "He's gonna have to share."

"Damn right," Kade said, pulling back just enough to meet her eyes, his thumb tracing her bottom lip. "You're mine, Mya. And I don't share."

Her smile was slow, wicked, and full of promise. "Good," she said, echoing his earlier words. "Because I don't either."

Inside, the clubhouse roared with laughter, the clink of bottles, the hum of brothers planning the next move. But out here, it was just them, the night stretching out, heavy with heat and unspoken vows. The war with the Reapers wasn't over, but with Mya's hand in his, her body pressed close, Kade knew he'd burn the world down before he let anyone touch her again.

Chapter Nine

Kade

Their clubhouse thrummed with the kind of tension that could snap bones. Cigarette smoke curled through the air, mixing with the sharp bite of whiskey and the faint metallic tang of gun oil. Outside, a late summer storm growled, thunder rolling like a warning from the gods. Inside, the brothers crowded around the scarred oak table in church, voices raised, tempers fraying like old leather.

Kade sat at the head, his knuckles white around a glass, his jaw tight enough to crack teeth. The warehouse raid had gutted the Reapers' drug pipeline, but the victory still tasted like ash. Rumors were spreading faster than the fire they'd set. Most indicated that Vance, the Reapers' President, was planning a hit, maybe at the Pets' charity run in two days. Kade's blood burned at the thought, his mind flickering to Mya, upstairs with the old ladies, her dark eyes haunted but defiant.

"We need to do it now. Something. Anything, brothers," Kade growled, slamming his fist on the table. "Vance wants to play dirty? We bury him before he gets the chance."

Dirteater leaned back, arms crossed, his weathered face skeptical. "Cops are already sniffing around, Prez. We move now, we're begging for a raid. We wait, let the dirty bastards come to us."

"Fuck waiting," Torch snapped from Kade's right, his shaved head gleaming under the fluorescent lights. "They're targeting the run. You want us to roll over like dogs? Like little bitches?"

The room split, half the brothers nodding with Torch, the others murmuring for caution. Kade's chest tightened, his gaze flicking to the ceiling as if he could see Mya through the floorboards. She was his weakness and his anchor, and the thought of Vance's hands on her made his vision red. The vote was close—too close—twenty-two to twenty for holding off. Kade shoved his chair back, the screech cutting through the din. Staying here wasn't what he wanted, but the vote was put to the members for a reason.

We're pausing, not backing away.

Torch was going to engage with their usual informants, and they'd have that info in a couple of hours.

I can wait to balance the scales for that long.

***

Mya

Upstairs, Mya paced the cramped lounge where the old ladies gossiped over beers. The muffled shouts from the men's meeting bled through the walls, words like "retaliation" and "mole" slicing into her thoughts. She wasn't some fragile thing to be locked away, no matter what Kade thought. The charity run was her chance to prove it, to show she could stand in his world. When Kade stormed upstairs, his eyes dark with fury, she met him in a quiet corner, her chin lifted.

"I'm helping with the run," she said, voice steady despite the storm in his gaze. "I'm not hiding."

"You're a target, Mya," he snapped, stepping close, his hand wrapping around her wrist—not hard, but firm. "You think I'm letting you walk into a fucking ambush?"

She yanked free and with heat rising in her face, their mouths inches apart, told him, "You don't get to cage me, Kade. I chose this. I chose *you*."

His breath hitched, something raw flickering in his eyes. She identified anger, need, and finally fear. "You don't know what you're asking for."

"Then show me," she shot back, her voice low, daring. "Teach me."

The air crackled, their bodies close enough to feel the heat. His hand twitched, like he wanted to grab her again, pull her closer, but a shout broke the spell. A prospect, pale and wide-eyed, burst in. Half the club followed him into the room. "Found another burner phone at the gate. One message again."

Kade snatched the device from the prospect, countenance darkening as he read aloud: "*Keep her close, Kade. Walls have ears."

Had to be from Vance. The words sank like lead, hinting at a traitor in their ranks. Kade's eyes met Mya's, his protective instincts roaring. "Torch, you're on her at the run. No arguments," he said, ignoring her glare.

Later, in Kade's room at the clubhouse, a threatening storm outside rattled the windows. Mya stood by his bed, her arms crossed, her voice sharp. "You can't keep me in the dark. I'm not some damsel."

He stalked toward her, his hands inches away from framing her face, pinning her against the wall without touching her. "You think I want this? Dragging you into my shit?" His voice was rough, his breath warm against her lips. "I'd burn it all down to keep you safe."

Her fingers curled into his cut, tugging him closer, her defiance meeting his restraint. "Then trust me to stand with you."

The room shrank to just them, his hands sliding to her jaw, her pulse hammering under his thumbs. Their lips were a whisper apart, the air thick with unspoken promises. A phone buzzed, shattering the moment. Kade pulled back, cursing under his breath. The message was from Torch, reporting a suspicious bike near the clubhouse.

Around midnight, Kade and Torch stood at the clubhouse gate, rain spitting against their cuts. A lone rider watched from the hill, silhouette stark against a lightning flash. The bike's engine roared, then faded as the rider peeled out. Kade's gut twisted. The Reapers were circling, and they were closer than he feared.

Chapter Ten

Kade

The charity run was a beast of noise and chrome, dozens of bikes tearing through the city's outskirts, their rumble drowning out the cheers of locals lining the streets. Rain slicked the asphalt, the air heavy with wet earth and exhaust. Kade led the pack, Mya's arms locked around his waist, her warmth a tether against the chaos in his head. She rode like she belonged, her chin high, her presence a middle finger to the Reapers' threats.

Every brother was armed, riding heavy while all eyes scanned for trouble. This run was for a local shelter for battered women, raising funds to expand the available services. What was meant to be a supportive moment of goodwill now carried tension like a blade at their throats. Whispers of Vance's retaliation had spread, and Kade's grip on the throttle tightened every time he caught a stranger's stare in the crowd.

Halfway through, at a gas station stop, trouble hit. As the main column of riders had already pulled back out on the road, a pack of Reapers rolled up, their cuts boldly carrying their patch. No shots were fired, but they swarmed a prospect, ripping his bike's keys and leaving a spray-painted WRMC tag on the pavement before they fled. When Dirteater relayed the information Kade's blood boiled, but he ordered a detour, his voice tight over their comms. "We ride on. No blood today."

Mya's hand squeezed his shoulder, steadying him. He reached back, his gloved fingers brushing hers, a fleeting caress. She didn't flinch, didn't waver, and it made his chest ache with something he couldn't name.

Back at the clubhouse, the mood was a strange mix of defiance and celebration. The run had raised good money, thousands of dollars for the shelter. The brothers toasted with cheap beer and loud laughter. Mya moved among the old ladies, pouring drinks, her smile cutting through the haze. Kade watched her from across the room, his beer untouched, his gaze heavy with pride and a hunger he couldn't shake. When her eyes met his, the noise faded, the crowd blurring. She crossed to him, her hips swaying just enough to make his jaw clench.

"You're staring," she teased, leaning close, her breath warm against his ear.

"You're making it hard not to," he growled, his voice low, meant for her alone.

In the back hallway, away from the chaos, he pulled her aside, his hands finding her hips, pressing her against the wall. "My Mya. Woman, you're gonna kill me with that stubborn streak," he said, his lips curling despite himself.

She smirked, her fingers brushing his chest. "You love it."

The air sparked, his hands tracing the curve of her waist, her breath catching as she leaned into him. Their lips brushed, a ghost of a kiss, but a shout broke them apart—Dirteater, holding a burner phone.

"Look at this shit." He thrust the phone into Kade's hand, Mya moving slightly behind him.

"What am I looking at?" He scrolled up and down the thread, putting the pieces together finally. "Who the fuck is this phone assigned to?" He glared at the multitude of texts linking a less-than promising hangaround to the Reapers.

"Mike Johnson, the little dicked prick." Dirteater shook his head. "Knew something wasn't right with that asshole. That's why my rock was black at the last vote."

"Do you know where he is?"

"Torch is organizing hauling him into the back room." Dirteater tipped his chin to the stairs. "I'm going down now."

"I'll be there in a few." Kade's words followed the Enforcer down the steps. He turned to Mya, seeing the acceptance in her face.

"No words needed, my man. Go, deal with the club's business, and then come back to me." Mya leaned close, offering her lips.

Kade took the invitation for a brief caress of their lips together before he pulled back. "I'll come back when I can."

Smiling, Mya lifted to her toes to glide her lips across his another time. "I'll be here."

***

Kade arrived downstairs about the time Mike Johnson lost the sneer off his face and started spewing information. Torch hauled the guy up off the floor and roared into his face, "You fucking dared to get our first lady nearly disappeared? And then you came back for more?" He shoved the man into Dirteaters waiting arms. It wasn't but another moment before even his last denials were sent crumbling under their glares.

They didn't learn much. Johnson had fed Vance small intel, just what they'd seen on the phone. But he swore he knew nothing about the attack on Kade and Mya's home.

Kade lounged against a wall, watching as Dirteater took the man to the floor. "Think that's all he knows?"

"Yeah. Fuckin' hangaround isn't smart enough to tell me any lies." Two right hooks rocked the man's head against the cement. "He's down for the count now. Tell me what we're doing with him."

"Gonna ban him. Gonna look deep at any prospect or hangaround he's been real friendly with. Gonna call the presidents of every fucking club within a five hundred mile radius and let him know he's persona non grata with the Pets." Kade shook his head, dropped the burner phone to the floor and stomped hard. Plastic shattered, the damage done music to Kade's ears. "Get a couple of prospects to haul his ass out of our clubhouse, give them the full story. I'd prefer everyone know rather than some of the nosey ones playing telephone."

Dirteater snapped a salute. "You got it, K-Man."

Later, Kade found Mya by the upstairs bar, and pulled her close, his lips against her temple. "I'll end this," he whispered, his voice a vow. "No one touches you."

His phone buzzed, the screen lighting up with a text:

*You burned our house. We'll burn yours.

No sender, but the threat was clear. Kade's arm tightened around Mya, his eyes scanning the shadows. The Reapers were coming, and this time, it was personal.

~ ~ End ~ ~

THANK YOU SO MUCH FOR READING
Sidetracked Love!

I truly hope you enjoyed this little story about an entirely new cast of characters! I had a blast writing them.

~ML

ABOUT THE AUTHOR

Raised in the south, *Wall Street Journal* & *USA TODAY* bestselling author MariaLisa learned about the magic of books at an early age. Every summer, she would spend hours in the local library, devouring books of every genre. Self-described as a book-a-holic, she says "I've always loved to read, but then I discovered writing, and found I adored that, too. For reading...if nothing else is available, I've been known to read the back of the cereal box."

Want sneak peeks into what she's working on, or to chat with other readers about her books? Join the Facebook group! **bit.ly/deMora-FB-group**

Sidetracked Love

deMora's got a spam-free newsletter list she'd love to have you join, too: **bit.ly/mldemora-newsletter**

~~~~~

My Rebel Wayfarers MC and the Neither This Nor That MC series do cross over, along with the Occupy Yourself band books, so readers have a couple of choices. The series can be read independently beginning with RWMC, OYBS, and then NTNT without too many spoilers. There's also a crossover between my RWMC world and Lila Rose's Hawks MC world. Or they can be read intertwined—in chronological order.

Here's the recommended reading order if you want to follow according to timing:

> *Mica*, RWMC #1
> *A Sweet & Merry Christmas*, RWMC #1.5
> *Slate*, RWMC #2
> *Bear*, RWMC #3
> *Born Into Trouble*, OYBS #1
> *Jase*, RWMC #4
> *Gunny*, RWMC #5
> *Mason*, RWMC #6
> *Hoss*, RWMC #7
> *This Is the Route of Twisted Pain*, NTNT #1
~~~~~

Harddrive Holidays, RWMC #7.5
Duck, RWMC #8
Biker Chick Campout, RWMC #8.5
Watcher, RWMC #9
Treading the Traitor's Path: Out Bad, NTNT #2
Living Without, Lila Rose's Hawks MC: Caroline Springs #4
Shelter My Heart, NTNT #3
A Kiss to Keep You, RWMC #9.25
Gun Totin' Annie, RWMC #9.5
Secret Santa, RWMC #9.75
Trapped by Fate on Reckless Roads, NTNT #4
Bones, RWMC #10
Gunny's Pups, RWMC #10.25
Not Even A Mouse, RWMC #10.75
Road Runner's Ride, RWMC #12.5
Never Settle, RWMC #10.5
Fury, RWMC #11
Christmas Doings, RWMC #11.25
Gypsy's Lady, RWMC #11.5
Tarnished Lies and Dead Ends, NTNT #5
Going Down Easy
No Man's Land
In Search of Solace
Cassie, RWMC #12

~~~~~

Also by MariaLisa deMora
~~~~~

Neither This Nor That MC romance series

Legends are born from moments like these. Folktales spun around a single point in time so perfect, you can almost hear the click resonating through the universe as things align. Meet Twisted, Po'Boy, Retro, and Ragman, good old boys from southern states who have many things in common. First, is a bone-deep love of the biker lifestyle. Second, would be their love of the brotherhood, and knowing that you trust the man at your back. Finally, these men have the love of a good woman. None of these come without a price, and it is our pleasure to journey along with them as they discover the blessings that can be won, and lost along the way.

This is the Route of Twisted Pain
Treading the Traitor's Path: Out Bad
Shelter My Heart
Trapped by Fate on Reckless Roads
Tarnished Lies and Dead Ends

5-Star Reviews for the stories of the NTNT MC series

This is the Route of Twisted Pain
"This is the Route of Twisted Pain is an exhilarating, gripping romance novel contrived of incredible world building, complex yet relatable characters, and a unique, captivating plot.
Gifted storyteller MariaLisa deMora beautifully balances exciting suspense, fast action, intriguing secrets with delicious, blazing hot romance scenes.
Readers will be up all night with this riveting page-turner."
~ NY Literary Magazine

I am completely tickled in my fancy for TWISTED!
First off, let me state that there was one thing I didn't like about this book and that is the LAST PAGE! I hated for it to end. I dearly loved this book and its characters as well as their setting.
~Colleen M.

Gripping tale
Twisted and Penny fit together beautifully. The book covers so much more than just their love story. Great introduction to the Incoherent MC. The tale is gripping and gritty. The journey is full of twists and turns that keep you on the edge of your seat. I couldn't put it down. Cannot wait for the next one.
~Lillmil

Sidetracked Love

Twisted is one of the most original and interesting characters I have read in a long time. Marialisa's character building is setting a high bar for her to follow, she will hopefully continue with Po'Boy's story. The Route of Twisted Pain was pure brilliance, and I highly recommend this read.
~Penny T.

This book obsessed me!
This may be the best book I read all year.
These people...they're not characters, they're real... have stuck in my head from the day I met them.
MariaLisa deMora can throw words down that'll Twist (hehe) your insides up till you can't breathe for waiting to hear what's next!
I'm working my way through her other 'families' and yup....she really is that good.
~DeLane

Treading the Traitor's Path: Out Bad
"Treading the Traitor's Path: Out Bad is a solidly engrossing, well-written novel by a talented author.
MariaLisa deMora delivers a thrilling ride filled with exciting suspense, deliciously explicit, vivid sex scenes, and gritty, fast-paced action. Her characters are smart, complex, and strong with sharp edges. The settings meticulously detailed. Fans of Motorcycle Club romance stories will not want to miss this second installment in

deMora's exciting series."
~ NY Literary Magazine
What an amazing read! DeMora does not
simply wrote a book, she pulls you into a
different world. When you read her work, you
are very much surrounded by the characters
and setting. Prepare for a book hangover
because once you finish the book, you will still
be stuck with Po Boy.
~KW

THIS WAS AMAZING. Highly recommend for a
good story line, interesting characters. I just
wish there was more more more.
~Laura

Loved This Book!
What did I just read?! Is my kindle still working?
I'm pretty sure it combusted into flames while
reading this story. RED HOT READ for 2017. Not
what I was expecting at all! I tend to stay away
from ménage a trois, because for me it's hard to
say there's any kind of conflict except for
jealousy, and the ending kind of leaves things
unresolved and unrealistic. NOT THIS BOOK!
The best one out there guaranteed.
~Linda A

...seriously this series is just WTF so freaking
good. Dark, Twisted, harsh, painful and raw.
Po'Boy lives for his club, his brothers and his

family, there is nothing he wouldn't do for them.
~Fay

I live and breathe for books like this! Fabulously Naughty!...Wickedly Hot! This is my first book by MariaLisa deMora and it will not be my last. MariaLisa delivered a 5 STAR READ! The plot is filled with action, suspense, romance and tons of hot scenes.
~Jenny F

~~~~~

Alace Sweets, a dark romantic suspense 3-book series

A dark thriller, this book is not a light read. Filled with edge-of-your-seat suspense, this intense story commands the reader's attention as it drives towards the explosive ending. Alace Sweets is a vigilante serial killer, with everything that implies and is sure to trip all your triggers. Be ready.
~~~~~

At seventeen, Alace Sweets turned a corner in her life, taking the wrong shortcut home from school.

Resisting the harsh knowledge her attackers will never be made to pay for their actions, Alace takes a stand. Justice must be served, and if fate's scales are out of balance, she's determined to set things right as best she can.

When the laws of men fail, the rules of Alace prevail.

5-Star Reviews for Alace Sweets

"Whatever deep dark trench [deMora] pulled a character like Alace from should be revisited again and often."
~Confessions of a Serial Reader

"deMora has a superb story-line and exceptional character development. All of her characters have such depth that will intrigue the reader..."
~Turning Another Page

"Hot, sweet, dark thriller."
~Beth D

Sidetracked Love

"It will keep you on the edge of your seat and give you chills."
~Escape Reality Book Blog

"Disturbing, haunting, sickly; yet hot, sexy and heart racing!"
~Amanda L

"From the first page [deMora] pulls you into the world she has created and you do not even try to escape…"
~Little Shop of Readers Blog

"A must read for all those dark, gritty romance fans out there."
~Sweet & Spicy Reads

"You will find yourself so drawn into the story that the outside world is blocked out and your locking the doors and turning on all the lights."
~Danena F

"Don't judge me for bonding with a vigilante serial killer, she's more than what she does."
~iScream Books

"Thrilling…chilling…full of suspense, nail biting edge of your seat excitement."
~Tracey H

"Every time MariaLisa deMora picks up her pen (or opens her computer), she creates characters you want to believe in."
~Gail S

"Intriguing dark storyline, beautiful love story and nail-biting conclusion, what more could a reader ask for?"
~Manda M

"This book takes you a dark and twisted ride that is gripping..."
~Renee Entress' Blog

"This book is dark and gritty and I literally had to take a day off from reading it because it's that intense."
~My Girlfriend's Couch

"This is my favourite book so far from this author ... I recommend this book if you enjoy dark romantic thrillers."
~Cheekypee Reads and Reviews

"There's not enough stars to give this book and 5 just doesn't really do it justice!"
~DeLane C

"I couldn't put this book down from page one! Tried to stop & go to bed but couldn't sleep thinking about Alace and got up & finished the book."

Sidetracked Love

~Debbie M

"MariaLisa DeMora, wordsmith that she is, made this a story of the enlightenment of a woman and finding love in a life where she has had none."
~Kat W

ADDITIONAL SERIES AND BOOKS

Please note that books in a series frequently feature characters from additional books within that series. If series books are read out of order, readers will twig to spoilers for the other books, so going back to read the skipped titles won't have the same angsty reveals.

Rebel Wayfarers MC series:

Mica, #1
A Sweet & Merry Christmas, #1.5
Slate, #2
Bear, #3
Jase, #4
Gunny, #5
Mason, #6
Hoss, #7
Harddrive Holidays, #7.5
Duck, #8
Biker Chick Campout, #8.5
Watcher, #9
A Kiss to Keep You, #9.25
Gun Totin' Annie, #9.5
Secret Santa, #9.75
Bones, #10
Gunny's Pups, #10.25
Never Settle, #10.5
Not Even A Mouse, #10.75
Fury, #11

Sidetracked Love

Christmas Doings, #11.25
Gypsy's Lady, #11.5
Cassie, #12
Road Runner's Ride, #12.5

Occupy Yourself band series:

Born Into Trouble, #1
Grace In Motion, #2 (TBD)
What They Say, #3 (TBD)

Neither This, Nor That MC series:

This Is the Route Of Twisted Pain, #1
Treading the Traitor's Path: Out Bad, #2
Shelter My Heart, #3
Trapped by Fate on Reckless Roads, #4
Tarnished Lies and Dead Ends, #5

Rebel Wayfarers crossover stories:

Going Down Easy
No Man's Land
In Search of Solace
Puppy Love
Steel and Swagger

Mayhan Bucklers MC series:

Most Rikki-Tik, #1

MariaLisa deMora

Mad Minute, #2
Pucker Factor, #3
Boocoo Dinky Dau, #4

Borderline Freaks MC series:

Service and Sacrifice, #1
More Than Enough, #2
Lack of Inbetween, #3
See You in Valhalla, #4

Alace Sweets series:

Alace Sweets, #1
Seeking Worthy Pursuits, #2
Embarrassment of Monsters, #3
All the Broken Rules, #4

With My Whole Heart series:

With My Whole Heart, #1
Bet On Us, #2

**If You Could Change One Thing:
Tangled Fates Stories**

There Are Limits, #1
Rules Are Rules, #2
The Gray Zone, #3

Other Books:

Outlaw Heartstrings
Sidetracked Love
Only For You
Hard Focus
Salvaged Parts
Spark of the Lock
Dirty Bitches MC: Season 3

More information available at **mldemora.com**.